THE OUTLIERS

THE OUTSKIRTS DUET, BOOK 2

T.M. FRAZIER

PROLOGUE

Love.

It isn't logical.

It doesn't grow or shrink on demand.

It's unexpected. Unyielding.

Love can be your greatest lover or your greatest enemy.

It makes no apologies when it feeds off the lie of forgiveness.

Love will fight the world even if it has no chance of winning.

It's the excuse and the reason.

The sacrifice and the reward.

The pain and the disappointment.

Love.

The ultimate betrayal.

CHAPTER 1

SAWYER

M y mother was standing a few feet away.
My *mother.*

Living. Breathing.

I couldn't catch my breath. My mind raced with possibilities, none of which made any sense.

I mean, it looked like her. But it also didn't look like her. It was something in her eyes, or maybe, something lacking in her eyes.

She took a small shuffled step toward me but since I didn't know what the proper protocol was when a ghost tries to touch you I leapt backward and knocked over a chair behind me, almost going down with it.

I was in an alternate universe. That had to be it. One where people came back from the dead. This couldn't of been real. Maybe it was all a dream. Or maybe it was the whiskey.

Disbelief, doubt, and utter confusion were mashing together in my gut, pushing upward on my racing heart and snaking its way into my tight throat.

I was afraid that if I blinked she would go away. I was afraid that if I didn't blink she *wouldn't* go away.

I—I couldn't do much of anything except gape at the woman who looked and sounded exactly like my mother. Only—it couldn't have been.

Could it?

"It's not possible," I said in a shocked whisper. "It's just not." I shook my head, wondering if I'd gone crazy before or after arriving in Outskirts.

"It's possible. She's really here." Critter's deep baritone voice was usually calming—the vocal equivalent of aloe vera. But in that moment there wasn't anything he could've said to stop hands from shaking or my palms from sweating.

"This ain't no dream, Sawyer. She's here. She's just as alive as you and me." I glanced up at him to find him watching me—gauging my reaction. "I told her she needed to hold off until she was stronger, but she wanted to see you and when she's all there, like she was this morning, there is no talking her out of it."

A tall, robust woman with broad square shoulders and short black hair appeared at my mother's side. The scowl on her face didn't match the bright pink scrubs with large, happy face print. "This is not good for her, Mr. Critter," the woman said. "I need to take her back to the house."

It was then I realized my mother hadn't moved since she'd first said my name. Her stare was blank and unfocused on the back wall.

"No, wait!" I called out. Suddenly I was more afraid I'd never get the chance to see her again, than I was of touching a ghost. And what if she was a ghost? What if this was all a dream? It didn't matter. She was still my mother and I couldn't let her go. Not yet. Not even in a dream.

I threw my arms around her and much to my surprise I connected with soft warm flesh.

My mother's arms were limp at her side, hanging lifelessly against her body. "My girl," she whispered.

I pulled back just in time to see a small smile form on her lips. It faded into a straight line just as quickly as it had appeared.

"What's wrong?" I asked on a strangled cry. Mother didn't answer. I turned to Critter. "What's wrong with her!" I demanded to know.

"Come on. It's time to go," the nurse said, scooping my mother up and cradling her in her arms like she weighed no more than a small child.

"What was I supposed to do, Maddy? Tie her to the goddamn bed?" Critter asked the nurse. "Never could say no to her." He grumbled, rubbing his temples.

"What's going on?" I demanded, glancing between the nurse and Critter. I took a step back while my mind raced. I held onto a table when I grew dizzy. "How is this possible?"

My mother moaned, and the nurse carried her out the back door. i followed with Critter close behind. We watched as the nurse placed my mother into an awaiting van, expertly buckling her into her seat.

Critter walked up to the open door and the nurse moved to make room for him. He stroked his hand lovingly over my mother's face. "It's okay. We'll get you home now so you can rest."

My mother didn't respond. "I'll come see you later,

my love." Critter kissed her on the forehead, sighed, then turned back to Maddy. "Take her home. I'll follow soon." He shut the door gently and rapped on the window. He watched the van take off, and was still watching it long after it had disappeared from sight.

"Where is she taking her?" I asked, feeling panic coursing through me at the idea of not knowing where she'd be as they drove off. "Where is home?"

"Home is my house," Critter answered, before quickly correcting himself. "*Our* house." He scratched his head and finally turned around. "Where she was always meant to be."

Where she was meant to be.

Critter placed a hand on my shoulder. I jumped back as if he'd shocked me instead of trying to comfort me. He looked to the ground. "I know you have a lot of questions..."

"Questions?" I asked, and without realizing it I started to laugh. A high pitched awful sounding laugh like a sound you'd hear an animal make at night but couldn't tell exactly what kind of animal. "Questions seems much too small of a word right now."

"I'm sorry I didn't tell you when you first got here," Critter continued, ignoring my outburst. "But your mother was in such rough shape that I didn't want you to have to grieve her twice if things didn't...if she... fuck." He took a deep breath. "I never gave any thought to the condition she'd be in when I got her back. I was stupid enough to assume she'd just be herself like she'd been before. I should have known better. You don't spend two decades with a man like Richard Dixon and come out whole on the other end." He looked at me and winced, realizing what he'd just said. "I'm sorry, I didn't mean...you, your..."

"Don't be sorry. That's the only part of all this that makes sense to me right now. You're right. You don't spend two decades with a man like him and come out whole." I took in a long shaky breath. "I'm all too familiar. But please tell me, what's wrong with her? How is she here?"

"It turns out she's suffering from post-traumatic stress disorder. It's the same thing soldiers sometimes go through after they've come home from combat. And there's no doubt in my mind that what your mother went through was a goddamned war zone. She was quiet, but all right at first. Mostly she just asked about you. Called your name over and over again in the middle of the night. Once we told her you were here and safe it was like all the walls she'd put up came crumbling down, and the magnitude of everything hit her like a damned tidal wave."

"Will she get better?" I asked.

Critter's eyes watered. He blew out a long breath. "Only time will tell. She's getting help. But she has her moments. Sometimes, when she's with it, she goes back and forth between the present and thinking it's twenty years ago."

"You lied to me," I blurted. Once the words left my lips I regretted it. It was the smallest of my concerns yet for some reason my brain placed it first.

"Yes, I did," Critter admitted. There was no apology. No regret in his voice. "But if it helps any, I know how you feel. I thought she was dead. I thought she'd left me and then he'd killed her." He clenched and unclenched his fists. "I know now that's just what he wanted me to believe. Your mother thought the same. That I was dead. Wasn't until I had a dream about her that I felt like she was somehow alive. I sent a team to look for her again. Some vet friends of mine that specialized in that sort of thing. At first, they didn't come up with a damn thing. And then they located the camper and truck in a storage unit in North Carolina. That's how I traced it back to her. That's how I knew where she was."

"She faked her own death?" I asked. It didn't sound right. She left me that box. That note. The truck and the camper. She practically admitted to taking her own life.

Critter looked to the ground and shuffled his feet. "No, she didn't fake her death. We did. She didn't know anything about it or even that I was alive."

"But then why did she write me a letter apologizing for killing herself? that doesn't make sense."

Critter shivered like someone had placed an ice cube at the base of his neck. "The plan was to get both of you out, but on the day we planned to carry it all out I was watching her from a distance. Waiting for the both of you to cross the street. But she was alone. Something was off. She wasn't just sad. There was something else there. A finality in the way she watched the traffic move back and forth on the road. I picked up my radio and called the boys. We made it look like she'd gone through with her intentions. Got some not so up-and-up members of society to do our bidding for us. They bribed everyone in that town seven ways 'til Sunday, until your mother was dead in every single sense but in the one that mattered. The breathing sense."

"This is all...it's crazy."

"That it is." Critter agreed, lighting a cigar. "We'd planned on coming back for you a few days later. I wouldn't have left you there. You need to know that. But by then you'd already bolted. I damn near had a fucking heart attack when you showed up at the bar that day."

"All this time I'd been here in Outskirts, she's...she's been here too?" I asked in a whisper.

Critter nodded without taking his eyes off me. His busy brows were furrowed, the lines on his face deepened to creases.

"And...and you've been caring for her?" I asked, already knowing the answer.

Another small nod.

Suddenly, the urge to catch my breath was overwhelming. My chest was tight. My throat dry. I couldn't swallow like something was stuck in my windpipe. I rubbed my arms like I could calm the flow of unease and confusion coursing through my entire body. I was cold and then hot. Nauseous.

Overwhelmed and dizzy, I gasped for breath.

I had to get out of there. Leave. Go...somewhere. Somewhere less confusing. Anywhere else.

Without another word, I turned and darted from the bar. I ran into the rain which had just begun to fall.

I should've been elated that my mother was alive and I was, but there was something else preventing that feeling from truly registering. A deep sense of hurt. A betrayal.

I ran faster and faster. The rain fell harder, stinging my skin with each step.

I used to fear storms. The thunder. The rain. Lightning. Wind. Then Finn taught me how to push through that fear and use it as a reminder to find the beautiful in something that can appear so ugly and cruel.

But as the rain continued to pour down all around me, soaking through my clothes and skin, it wasn't a reminder. It didn't provoke any fear or any emotion at all.

It was just rain. Just water.

Because my mother was alive.

CHAPTER 2

SAWYER

Finn is hovering above me in bed, his body is pressed against mine in the most delicious way. The heat from his chest warming my heart as well as my skin. His blond hair is disheveled. A light sheen of sweat covers his lightly tanned skin. His defined shoulder muscles are strained with tension.

I run my hand over his bristly jaw, and he closes his eyes like my touch is everything to him, and in that moment, I feel like it is. He peers down at me with his beautiful bright blue eyes and it's like he's looking so deeply into mine that he can see right through me when he thrusts inside me for the first time. My body ignites, and he groans, pulling out and pushing inside my body all over again. He kisses me, drinks in my lips like he's dying of thirst and I moan his name into his mouth as our tongues meet.

"I love you," he whispers.

I'm trembling. With joy. With anticipation. He's everything I never knew I needed. My heart expands and my sex *clenches around him as he thrusts harder and deeper inside my swollen channel.*

I'm so close. The buildup is almost painful. Every stroke leaves me needier than the last.

Finn drives into me faster and faster. Relentlessly pounding harder and harder. Just as I reach the edge of my release...he's gone. The bed's gone. I'm now standing behind a familiar crowd of people in an even more familiar setting. Somewhere I never wanted to be the first time around.

"Marriage is the most sacred promise you can make. Family is second only to God himself." The Reverend preaches from behind his podium of lies. My mother's casket is front and center.

I'm back at her funeral.

Only, something's different.

Off.

Everyone in the crowd is smiling. They keep looking over their shoulders like they are all waiting for something.

Finn comes into view and I'm instantly relieved to see him. I exhale. He's as handsome as ever, wearing a dark grey suit with matching tie. His eyes crinkle slightly at the edges as his smile grows bigger and brighter. My stomach flutters. He walks down the aisle and just as he approaches I realize he's not looking AT me. He's looking THROUGH me.

Finn passes me by and stops at the podium, standing next to the reverend who places a hand on his shoulder.

What is he doing here? What's going on? I wonder as I look down only to find I'm once again dressed in a long skirt and shapeless grey blouse.

I try to take a step, to reach for him but I can't. I'm frozen in place. I try and shout his name but no sound comes out.

He can't hear me. He's focused on something else down the center of the aisle.

Someone else.

A beautiful blond woman appears with perfect blonde hair and a bright white smile. She's wearing a long white wedding dress. A tear drips down her cheek as she reaches Finn who takes her hands in his. They only look at each other.

"We are gathered here before God to join Finn Hollis and Jacqueline Watson..."

Jackie.

I don't listen to the rest. I can't. I can't even breathe. My chest is terrifyingly tight it feels like someone is jumping on my chest.

I try and shout again, but it's not working. They can't hear me. Or at least Finn can't. Jackie looks over to me, her head turning ever so slowly.

She winks.

I gasp and back out of the tent. Knocking chairs over on my way. Once again stumbling over a headstone but this time when I use it to break my fall I notice the name on it.

Mine.

I turn and run. Faster and faster leaping over headstones until they turn into trees, the earth growing soggy beneath my feet.

I'm winded, but I push through the sharp burning sensation building in my lungs. The air is hot in my throat as I breathe through my mouth, trying to pull in as much oxygen as I can so I can keep going.

I have to keep going.

I hear the echo of footsteps running behind me.

I'm not alone.

I run faster and faster. The brush grows thicker and

thicker until my long skirt gets caught on a branch and drags me to a sudden halt. I fall forward onto the ground. My hands sting as I break my fall on a log. My teeth vibrate like a tuning fork when my chin smacks into the earth.

I turn and attempt to yank on my skirt in order to free it from the brush it's snagged on, but suddenly the thorns on the branch that has me captive turns into fingers. The fingers grow longer and longer, the flowers turn to hands, the branches to arms. Nightmarish flowers of flesh. Hundreds of them reach for me and I skid in the soft earth, trying to stand, to get away.

I unbutton my skirt and push it down my legs, but it's too late. The hands are holding me down against the ground. Struggling is useless. I'm trapped, my head encased in the flesh of the human finger flowers.

I try and scream as more and more sprout from nowhere, reach across my body, and strap me down like a crazy person to a gurney, but again, silence.

A small slit between fingers allows me to see the legs of the person who's been chasing me as they come to a stop.

My mouth is suddenly covered by a hand.

Then my nose.

I can't breathe as the person finally comes into full view.

Mother.

She glances down, shakes her head and smirks. Kneeling beside me she begins to laugh silently. Her mouth wide open, her shoulders shaking violently.

I wonder if I can't hear her because the hands are covering my ears.

Or because I'm already dead.

CHAPTER 3

FINN

A fter I saw the cavalry from the church begin to arrive I spent the entire afternoon watching them set up their tent and unload their trucks.

I grabbed my boat and when I got close enough, I killed the engine and paddled my way under an embankment where I sat quietly, listening to the workers setting up the tent service. I hadn't heard much more than shouted instructions. I was about to leave when I heard the voices of two men directly above me, walking along the edge of the embankment just a few feet above my head. I crouched as close to the muddy wall as I could.

"Who is delivering the Lord's word this season?" one man asked the other. My ears instantly perked. My heartbeat quickened.

"I think they are sending Pastor Young since Pastor Dixon won't be coming until later this season. If he comes at all he'll be at least a few weeks behind the rest of us."

"What a shame about his wife. God bless her."

"Yes, but the Lord has his reasons."

"Amen. Family is the light of the Lord. His will in human flesh."

The other man mumbled his agreement and then they were gone.

Thank fuck. Richard wouldn't be coming, but while I made my way back to land so I could get to Sawyer, I was filled with unease. He might not be coming now and I knew for a fact Critter still had eyes on him, but my relief was short term because he would always be a threat. We'd always be looking over our shoulders.

By the time I made my way back to my truck, I hadn't realized how long I'd been watching them when I checked my phone. Five missed calls. Two from the landline at Critter's bar and three from Critter himself.

I called Critter's cell.

Critter answered with a gruff, "What?"

"The church cavalry is in town, but I overheard some of the workers. Richard Dixon won't be joining them this year."

"Good. My guy will tell me if he so much as crosses over the state line, but right now we got bigger fish to fry. Sawyer knows about her mama."

"I thought you were going to wait."

"Yeah, but Caroline had a moment of clarity and all she wanted was to see her daughter. I thought it might help."

"Did it?"

There was a pause. "No. Not for either of them."

THE LIBRARY DOOR was unlocked and a single table light was on in the center of the room.

There was Sawyer, hunched over the table with a book underneath her arms, her wild hair spread out like the rays of an auburn colored sun.

I breathed out a heavy sigh of relief.

"I thought I'd find you here," I said, coming up behind her and leaning over her shoulder, breathing in her familiar lavender scent. "What are you doing?" I whispered, placing my chin on her shoulder.

She lifted her head, spun around and I took a step back. Immediately I noticed the tear stains on her face. Her swollen eyes. The redness of her cheeks. "I must have fallen asleep," she said, looking dazed and breathing hard. "I had a nightmare."

"Are you okay?" I asked, crouching down in front of her and taking her hands in mine. "I talked to Critter. He told me what happened with your mom. Are you alright?" I bent over and wrapped my arms around her, pressing my rough cheek to her soft one.

She shrugged slowly as if her shoulders were heavy under the weight of her troubles. "And then there was the bad dream I just had where you were...never mind."

"Tell me," I insisted.

She shook her head. "It's not important. I thought I was naive and that I didn't know a lot about the outside world, but as it turns out, I just don't know much about anything, including my past, including anything about my own mother. She's...she's alive, but she's not the same. Critter said it's something called Post Traumatic Stress Disorder. I want to be happy I do. I just...I can't. Not yet. It's all too much."

There is more.

Guilt immediately washed over me for keeping the truth from her. She deserved to know it all. "Say, I have to tell you something," I started, but she interrupted me.

"I couldn't imagine having a daughter and just vanishing on her. Letting her think I was dead when I wasn't. Not even for a second." She grabbed her stomach, wrapping her arms around herself in a hug like the thought was making her physically ill. In fact, it might have been making her ill because she looked a lot paler than usual. Her eyes were lined with dark circles.

"I'm just really confused. I don't know where to place all these feelings. The anger. The hurt. The...everything." Sawyer turned back around and dropped her head to her chest. My strong girl who'd faced the devil with horns of her own was flailing and I felt helpless when her shoulders shook.

"Hey," I said, wrapping my arms around her. "You're right, you know what? When you become a mother to our children, I know that you would never abandon them at any cost. Because that's who you are. Neither of us would ever do that. But you don't know everything yet. You need to talk to Critter. To your mother and..."

"Our children?" Sawyer asked with a sniffle.

My chest tightened. Out of all I was saying that's what she'd heard the loudest. "Yes. Our children. Together. Me and you." I cupped her face in my hand. "I'd like nothing more than to see you carrying our baby someday." And it was true. The very thought of Sawyer carrying my baby made my heart warm and a primal part of me want to pound on my chest and roar into the night. Since no precautions were taken, it was always a possibility.

Sawyer's smile was a tear-filled one. "Me too. Someday, I'd like that very much." The sadness in her voice made my heart lurch in my chest not being able to take away her pain.

I was holding her tight to my chest when she pushed away for a moment to pick up a familiar crumbled yellow flyer that had been shoved in the mail slot. I knew exactly what it was because Critter had shown it to me before.

This was Sawyer's first time seeing it. In Outskirts, at least. I held my breath as she scanned the flyer. Her eyes went wide. The logo for God's Light Church couldn't be missed.

"He's...he's here," she whispered. Unblinking she took a wobbly step back, knocking over a chair.

I reached for the flyer. Needing to take it away from her like it could also take away the fear written all over her face. "No. He's not here. Not yet."

Sawyer stumbled again. She righted herself before using one of the bookshelves. The flyer still in her hand she held it up in her balled-up fist. "How do you know that? You can't know that! He's here, and I won't let him take me. I won't! You don't know him. He'll find me. He'll try and break me the way he broke her!"

Sawyer turned away but I spun her back around to face me. I crouched down, ensuring my eyes were in line with hers so she could see the truth in my eyes if by chance she didn't hear it in my words. "I know he's not coming because I went there. To the fairgrounds. That's where I was tonight. I saw the trucks come in off the highway and I followed them."

Sawyer took a step back, and this time I let her have the space. It was only a few steps although now it felt like a canyon between us.

"And no one could break you. No one. You're far too strong to be broken by weak minded people. Look at all you've been through and how far you've come."

"I won't have it all taken away from me. Not when I just found this place. Not when I just found you."

I felt damned awful for leaving out the parts of the story that were--as Critter would say--not my story to tell. "I went there tonight, and I overheard some of the workers talking. Your father--Richard-- isn't coming. Not for a while anyway. We have time. We won't be here when he gets here. It will all be okay." I said, trying as much to convince myself as I was Sawyer.

Sawyer scoffed. "He'll want his revenge for the money I stole. He'll want his revenge for me running away. He'll kill me the way I'm sure he'd always planned to kill me because he blamed me when she died." A look of pure panic crossed over her face. "Wait, my mother! Does he know she's alive? She can't know? If he's not there, then where is he? Where is my father?" She placed her shaky fingers over her lips.

I cringed at the next answer I had to deliver to her. "He's not here. If he crosses the state line, we will know first. I'm going to protect you, Sawyer. I swear with everything I have that I will keep you safe."

"But he could come here. He could come for us." She gasped. "My mother!"

"Your mother is with Critter right now. She's safe. I

promise. He wouldn't let anything happen to her just like I would never let anything happen to you."

Sawyer shoulders visibly dropped until she straightened like she'd rethought whatever had her slumping over to begin with. "I'm going to go to the church," she said, marching toward the door. "I'm going to tell them what a monster he is. They may not value women but they can't turn a blind eye to all the harm he's caused. If they can use the Bible to justify their actions they can use it to see how wrong they are as well."

I pushed the door shut the second she opened it. "No, the fuck you won't. I'm going to keep you safe whether you like it or not and confronting an entire church of your father's supporters isn't in the plans."

"I have to do something! I can't just sit here like a cow in a pasture waiting for the butcher. I have to act. I must get to him first. I have to tell someone in the church about who he is and what he is capable of!" Her eyes were wild. Crazed. "I feel like a caged animal. There is no escape. There will never be an escape."

"Yes, there will be. But tell me this, what do you think is going to happen when you walk into that tent and accuse one of their own of things you yourself told me they may already know about. And even if they didn't condone that sort of thing why would they listen to you? You're a defector with no physical evidence to back up your claims. Who do you think they are going to believe?"

"You're right." She shook her head. Her face was splotchy patches of red and pink over her smattering of freckles. Her shoulders deflated. She ran her fingers through her hair and tugged at the roots. "I can't just wait for him to hurt us again. Not this time."

"We will figure something out. We will get a plan together but you best believe I'm not letting you do something bullheaded and brave if it puts you at any sort of risk."

"But I can do this!" she argued. "I can go stop him!"

"No!" I growled, backing her into a shelf. Books clattered to the ground.

"We've been through this, Finn. Don't treat me like I'm fragile. Like I'm going to break." She turned her back to me. "I'm not her. I'm not Jackie!"

"No. You're nothing like her," I said softly. Reaching for her, I gently grip her waist as if to remind her she wasn't alone anymore and never would be again. "You're strong, my love. So very strong."

"Then please stop treating me like you don't trust me to handle this when I've handled so much worse! I've seen worse. If we make decisions together then help me make this one," she argued.

I tipped her chin up until her eyes found mine. "No," I snapped, trying to keep my tone as soft as possible so she wouldn't confuse my assertiveness with anger. "That's not happening. I trust you. I do. I just want to keep you safe and I can't do that if—"

"You can't what, Finn?" Sawyer asked. She held out her arms like she was waiting to catch whatever answer I was going to throw at her. "Because whatever it is you must tell me, tell me, because I'm tired of these half-truths that have been fed to me my entire life."

"I can't fucking lose you!" I shouted, my words

22

echoed off the walls and ceiling, surrounding us in the desperation of my words.

She took a step back but I held her in place. I leaned down and gazed into the depths of her eyes. With all the determination I could muster, I told her the truth. Gentler this time. "I just can't lose you. I can't go through that again. Not with you. Not ever. I just fucking can't. Don't put me through that. I won't recover because I refuse to live without you."

The anger was instantly doused from her eyes and she leaned into me. I wrapped my arms around her and pulled her close. "You won't ever lose me," she said. "But you have to promise not to treat me like I'm made out of glass or thin paper when I'm—"

"When you're really made out of piss and vinegar," I finished her sentence for her.

"I have no idea what that means," she said with a small laugh and a sniffle.

"It means that you're a force to be reckoned with. I know that, Say." I brushed off a tendril of wild hair that had fallen into my eyes. "I knew it the first moment I saw you on that road and it was confirmed when you came walking through my clearing."

She stood on her tiptoes. Craning her neck, she smiled against the skin below my ear and whispered. "It's my clearing too."

My chuckle turned into an all-out laugh as I picked me up and carried her over to a table. "I was right." I brushed a quick kiss across her lips. "All piss and vinegar."

I cupped her cheek and she leaned into my touch. Her eyes were still watery. Sad. My heart lurched in my chest. "What can I do to make this better?" I asked, swiping my thumb over her tears.

"I saw the tings tonight. The ones you'd hung for me. Right before the whole...thing with my mother." She flashed me a sad smile. "Thank you."

"It was just the truth. I actually hung them weeks ago." I sucked in a deep breath. "I'd do anything for you, Say. Tell me, what I can do for you now? I hate seeing you like this."

Sawyer thought for a moment. "I just don't want to think about it right now. Any of it. I just want a second to breathe. To think about something else. To disappear from reality. To feel...anything else. Just for a little while." Fresh tears pooled in her eyes and I could feel the pain tightening in my chest.

Anger bubbled to the surface and I found myself clenching my fists to fight off this invisible beast of the past tormenting my girl from the inside out.

"Just take it away, Finn. Just take it all away," she whispered, placing her small hand on my chest and looked up at me with pleading eyes.

I sucked in a shaky breath. "Tell me, Say. Tell me what you want and it's yours," I whispered, pressing my lips against her neck right below her ear.

She trembled against me. The tiny hairs on her neck stood on end. Her quick intake of breath when I grazed my teeth over her skin made my pulse pound loudly in my ears. I trailed my lips to her jaw.

"I...I want..." she stammered.

"Tell me. Do you want me, Say? Do you want me to fuck you? Make you come hard that you'll forget everything, including your own name?" I threaded my fingers through her wild cascading hair. "I can do that. I can make your body feel so good that your mind can rest a while."

"Yes," she said on a moan. When our eyes connected, there was lust there as well as embarrassment at her confession when she looked away to her feet. Her face reddened.

"Look at me." I tilted her face up by her chin to make sure our eyes met once again.

She complied, but there was still hesitation in her gaze. Shame.

"What we do? Me and you?" I asked, pointing between us. "It's not shameful. The way we make each other feel? It's fucking beautiful. The most fucking beautiful thing I've ever experienced. Don't ever feel ashamed to tell me what you want. To ask me for it. I love that you want me, Say. Now, be a good girl and tell me to fuck you."

I took her wrist and guided her hand to the front of my jeans so she could feel for herself that what I was saying was true. "Feel for yourself what you do to me."

She sucked in a sharp breath.

"You wanting me to take away your pain for just a few minutes this way is the most precious gift you could ever give me and not just your body. Your trust." I placed a soft kiss on her eyebrow. Her temple. Her cheek.

Her pulse quickened.

"Thank you for trusting me," I whispered before kissing her lips until we were both moaning into one another's mouths. Her soft pink lips opened for me and her tongue greedily searched for mine as I snaked my hand up her thigh into her panties. Groaning when I found her soaking wet and ready for me, but I still needed to hear the words. " I'll give you what you need. Always. Just tell me what you want and it's yours."

"How?" she breathed, craning her neck to me. Our foreheads rested against one another as we breathed in each other's air. I was ready for her. To be with her. Inside of her. But I needed her to say the words.

"Repeat after me." I held her gaze. "I want you."

"I want you," she repeated on a whisper. I saw the raw desire in her eyes and I knew it mirrored my own.

She trembled and her eyes shut. "Look at me," I demanded. When she did, I kissed her again. Deeply, crazily. Like my life depended on keeping my mouth connected to her in some way.

I swallowed hard. "Good girl," I praised, nipping her earlobe into my mouth. I traced my thumb over her nipple through her shirt and her back arched, pushing her chest against mine. I chuckled against her neck. "Now say, Fuck me, Finn."

My eyes went to her throat where I could see her pulse quicken beneath her smooth skin. She twisted her pouty pink lips. Her hesitation only lasted a second before she wrapped her arms around my neck and pulled me down closer so that the tips of our noses touched. Her lips feathered against mine. "Fuck me, Finn."

"Yes," I growled.

I may have been the one who told her to say those words but hearing them out of her mouth caused the raging inferno of lust within me to explode beyond control. I had a feeling I'd be hearing those words on repeat in my head for the rest of my life.

Fuck me, Finn.

I lifted her up onto the nearest table and pushed her onto her back. I tore her panties off in one tug and while I devoured her with my eyes, I somehow managed to concentrate enough to unbuckle my belt and push my jeans down over my ass, freeing my throbbing cock.

Sawyer moaned when I parted her legs, stepping between them. The sound was pure fucking heaven. Our tongues danced while we drank each other in. I savored the way her body felt against mine. Hard against soft. I dug my fingers into the flesh of her perfectly round ass before moving them to her pussy where I parted her warm wet folds and strummed her swollen clit because Sawyer was my instrument of choice and only I knew how to play her to perfection.

The look on Sawyer's face when I inserted a finger inside of her was as if I'd just given her a drug. She was high on the pleasure. Her lids were heavy. Her pupils large and dark. I was dead set on making sure I wrung every bit of pleasure from her gorgeous body and I gave her exactly what she'd asked me for.

An escape.

And if anyone knew a thing or two about escape, it was me.

Sawyer writhed against my hand, dripping down my wrist. Her pussy tightened around me and I groaned, wishing I'd felt that on my cock. I hooked my arm around her waist and dragged her to the edge of the table. "Ride my hand," I ordered on a strangled rasp. Lost in sensation, she glanced up at me for only a second before she began rotating her hips against my hand which was still furiously fucking and strumming her in every place that made her moan.

Her eyes rolled back in her head when her first orgasm crashed over her. The sound of her screaming my name echoed across the room. Her pussy clamped around me so hard that I didn't know if I'd be able to pull my finger back out.

Fuck it. It didn't matter. I'd gladly keep it inside of her forever.

I pushed her back on the table again and parted her folds with the tip of my cock then again, I tugged her body down to sheath me in her tight pussy.

She tossed her head back and pressed her lips together. She must have become aware of how loud she'd been screaming after she came the first time because she was holding back on me.

"No one can hear you and who the fuck cares if they can? Let it out, Say," I rasped, seeing stars as I pushed through her clenched pussy until I was as deep as her body would allow. "This is me and you, remember? You can do no wrong. Scream. Shout. Claw. Bite. But don't hold back. Don't ever fucking hold back on me." I pulled out halfway then pushed back in with a hard thrust.

She opened her mouth and the most amazing sound came out. A half moan half scream that almost had me coming inside of her instantly. I felt dizzy from it. I wanted to record that sound and listen to it over and over again.

Sawyer had awakened feelings inside of me I never thought I'd feel again and it was like once she opened the bottle the lid could never be put back on. Because my desire for Sawyer, my love for her, was the strongest thing I'd ever felt. Each time we came together was better than the last. Each time it fused us together more and more and I knew by now that our future was the kind that only ended in forever.

Our eyes met as I found my rhythm. Each time I pushed in she'd buck against me, pulling me in deeper and deeper until I couldn't help but to pound harder until there was no discernible rhythm. Just pleasure and moans and the slapping of skin against skin. When I felt her clench around my cock, my vision went white. The pleasure shot up my spine and when she cried out and contracted around me over and over again, she milked every last drop of cum from my pulsing cock.

Along with every last drop of love from my heart.

I laid there, with my girl sleeping in my arms but I couldn't enjoy the moment. My gut told me that soon we'd both be wishing that our temporary reprieve from reality was a lot more permanent.

CHAPTER 4

FINN

W hen I woke up the next morning I reached for Sawyer, but the only thing I met was mattress. I sat up in bed and was met with the smell of bacon. I made my way out of the room to the small kitchen in her little house and was taken aback by the buffet that was waiting for me on the counter. Along with the bacon were scrambled eggs, toast, juice, coffee, and hash browns.

My stomach growled.

What surprised me more was Sawyer who still hadn't noticed my presence. I stood there for a few moments. Watching her. Observing. Not only was she cooking up a storm, flitting from one cabinet to the other to get what she needed, she was also humming along to the song on the radio.

This wasn't the same girl from last night. I was confused and felt on edge watching this new Sawyer prance around the kitchen.

"What's all this?" I asked.

She turned around and almost dropped a plate but recovered quickly before setting it down on the counter. "You startled me," she said with a big beaming smile and I knew right away that something was amiss. "I thought I was supposed to be the one who didn't know things. This is breakfast of course."

"I didn't mean to startle you," I said, coming up behind her and wrapping my arms around her. I planted a kiss on her head before releasing her. "And I can see this is breakfast, but I was talking more about the humming and cooking and your overall demeanor, not the food." I grabbed a piece of crispy bacon and took a bite, my eyes almost rolled back in my head with the salty goodness.

"I like this song. The singer's name is Beyoncé. Have you heard of her?" Sawyer asked. She pronounced Beyoncé (Bee-Yon-Chee) and I couldn't help but smile.

"I think I might have heard of her once or twice," I answered, taking a seat at the counter. "But what I meant was, last night, you were pretty upset, and now?" I gestured to the counter and to the radio.

She smiled but it was a forced smile that barely more than a line on her face. "Nothing. I'm going to work," she said with a shrug. And that's when I saw it. The void in her eyes. The vacant space where so much life used to live. It was like she was running on idle.

"Work?" I asked. I shook my head. "Not today. Today you need to go talk to Critter about your mom. Maybe, go see her."

Sawyer averted her eyes shook her head. She set a pan in the sink and turned off the faucet. "No. Not yet. Not today."

"Say, you can't just go about your day as if last night never happened. It's a lot to take in. I think you can take the day off."

She looked at me as if I were the one acting strangely. "Right now, I'd rather focus on this. Breakfast. Being happy." She looked at me. "With you."

I leaned in and pressed a kiss to her lips. "I love that you want to be happy with me because fuck all knows that's all I want in the world. But I know how it goes when you push that shit down deep inside instead of letting it out and you know what happens?"

"You wind up living with the crazy girl from a religious sect in the middle of the swamp?" she asked, pressing a kiss to my jaw.

"Cute. But seriously, back up, 'cause that shit don't work. Trust me. Go talk to Critter. To your mother," I said, feeling more than just a little uneasy about her playful attitude when just last night she was about to lose her shit. "You can't just ignore this, Say."

"Sure," she said, planting another kiss on my lips. She grabbed her bag and slung it over her shoulder. "Just not yet."

"You're infuriating. Hang on, at least let me drive you," I offered, grabbing my t-shirt from the chair and tossing it on over my head.

"That's okay. Stay. Eat. I can walk. Besides, I told Josh I'd stop by her place before my shift."

"Just as a reminder we still don't know if it's safe," I said, pulling on my shirt and grabbing my keys. "Until then you're not walking anywhere alone."

"It's not a big deal," she said, reaching for the door. "You don't have to walk me. I can take care of myself."

"Yes." I stood in her path. "But you don't have to. You're not going anywhere. Not alone. I meant it when I told you that I can't lose you." The fear raging inside of me was so real it was almost tangible. If only she could feel a fraction of what I was feeling she'd understand the reason for my demands.

It's only because I'm terrified of losing you.

"You're not my mother, Finn," she said with a vacant expression on her beautiful face that made me want to punch a hole through the wall.

"No. I'm not." I leaned against the wall, crossing my legs at the ankles. I shrugged. "Why don't you go talk to her?"

"Cute," she said, throwing my earlier word back at me.

"I'm serious, Say. There are still things you need to know. Things up until this morning I thought you'd always wanted to know. Like why your mother owned land here. Like why..."

"Like why Critter is married to her?"

"Let me guess, because it's not your story to tell?"

"B-I-N-G-O."

Sawyer scrunched up her face in confusion and I took that to mean she didn't understand my reference. "I mean, you're right. It's not my story to tell. And FYI, emotional robot position? It's not for you. Why don't you bring my girl back."

She sighed. "What if it's all too much?" she asked, her lower lip quivering. As much as I hated to see her upset I was glad to see some emotion from her. "What if I can't handle what I learn. What if they tell me something I can't unhear? Something that will follow me around for the rest of my life? I don't know if I can handle that."

I kissed the top of her head. "She's your mother. You thought she'd abandoned you and she didn't. She's here now. She's alive. Most people don't get second chances like this. People don't come back from the dead but she did. Don't you think you owe it to her to hear her out? To hear Critter out?"

She nodded against my chest but her shoulders remained stiff. She was scared and she had every right to be, but I needed her to know she wasn't going to go through this alone.

"Say," I said, pulling away so I could look in her eyes. "You have me. Don't you know by now that I'd do anything for you? When the world gets heavy on your shoulders I'll carry the weight for you. I'll be there. I'm not going anywhere. Not now. Not ever."

Sawyer's lips turned upward in a smile. It was small but at least it was real. She sniffled. "Take me to her."

I sighed in relief but it wasn't a full breath. While Richard was still out there and Sawyer and her mom were here I'd never be able to fully relax. I pulled her back against me and rested my chin on top of her head. I wasn't lying when I told her I'd carry the weight of the world on my shoulders for her.

What I didn't mention was the possibility it might crush us both.

CHAPTER 5

SAWYER

Critter's house was a red ranch style home with a beige stucco exterior and black shutters encasing the two small front windows. I didn't know what to expect of his house, but what I didn't expect was for it to be sitting in a field of sunflowers.

I touched the sunflower pendant hanging from my neck. The one my mother had left for me in the box beneath my bed.

I remained in the car as Finn got out and opened my door. "Are you ready?" he asked me, helping me down and squeezing my hand tightly.

"I don't think I'll ever be," I answered. Finn led me up to the front porch where Critter was sitting on one of two wicker rocking chairs. He didn't waste any time. "Sawyer, I understand you're confused, but remember, so is she. Your mother has got some moments of clarity. Sometimes they last minutes and sometimes hours. Most of the time she thinks it's twenty-two years ago."

"I'm not going to upset her," I promised. "At least, I'll try not to."

Critter nodded to me and I turned to Finn. "I think I need to do this alone," I said.

"I'll be right out here waiting," he said, kissing my knuckles before releasing me. Critter opened the screen door for me. "Last door at the end of the hall."

My eyes adjusted to the darkness inside the cozy home with plush carpet and a million picture frames on the wall. It reminded me of a homier version of the bar.

When I got to the room at the end of the hall, I half expected my mother to be lying in bed but instead she was sitting on a rocking chair in the corner, knitting. Her nurse, Maddy, was sitting on another chair nearby flipping through a magazine. Maddy lifted her head when she saw me and gave me a warning look.

"Critter said it was okay," I told her.

She looked to my mother and then back to me. "Caroline, you've got a visitor," she said loudly yet sweetly. "Best way not to upset her is don't correct her if she says something that doesn't sound right and don't remind her of who you are because chances are, with how she's doing right now, she's not gonna know." With that Maddy left the room and closed the door behind her.

"Hello, there, dear. What's your name?" my mother asked when she noticed me standing at the end of the bed. She set her knitting down. A tangle of baby pink yarn with no decipherable pattern. Her blonde hair was wet and neatly combed back. She wore a pink fluffy bathrobe over pink and white striped pajamas, complete with fuzzy slippers. It was the most color I'd ever seen her wear besides the yellow tank top in the picture I'd found in the box she'd left for me. She looked healthy. Heavier.

Stronger than I'd seen in years.

Physically anyway.

"Hi," I said, feeling odd not knowing how to introduce myself to my own mother. I searched her face for any signs of recognition.

Nothing.

I ignored the growing pit in my stomach and ache in my heart.

"I'm...Sawyer."

She set her knitting down on her lap. "You must be the neighbor Critter was talking about. The new one with the little boy who keeps stealing all the sunflowers. It's nice to finally meet you."

"Nice to meet you too," I said, sitting down on the edge of the bed where the nurse had been. "And I'm sorry about him stealing your flowers."

"Oh, that's all right. We'll find out how mischievous children can be soon enough. Sorry I can't fetch you something to drink. Critter has been real insistent that I stay put since the morning sickness has really been getting to me."

"Morning sickness?" I asked. "You're pregnant?"

My mother removed the knitting and smoothed her hand over her flat stomach like it was rounded instead of indented. "Yes, six months along now and the sick feeling still hasn't subsided. Sometimes I think my daughter will be out into the world and full grown by the time it goes away."

"I'm sorry you aren't feeling well," I said, "But I'm sure Critter is taking good care of you."

"That man would lasso the moon if I asked him to. That's why I married him."

"Married?" I asked.

"Yep, right before we found out we were having a baby. It was low-key, just us in the sunflower field with a justice of the peace from the county office. I don't have a lot of family and neither does Critter. It was more special that way. Although, it won't be that way for long." My mother was beaming as she rocked and continued to knit.

"So, tell me, how did you two meet?" I asked casually, trying to seem like a curious neighbor.

"Well, it was love at first sight. I was..." she scrunched her face and shook her head like she was shaking off a bad memory. "You don't want to hear all this from me, do you? It's kind of a long story."

"I do. I really do," I urged her on, trying not to show the nervousness wreaking havoc on my heart.

I was finally going to hear the story I'd waited so long for. Part of me wanted to turn and run. Another part of me wouldn't move if a bulldozer came through the wall.

"From the beginning, if you'd like," I offered. "The very beginning. Your beginning. I've got plenty of time." I looked at my naked wrist like I was checking the time on a watch when I'd never even owned one. I slid to the floor and brought my knees to my chest with my back against the bed and tried not to tap my toe on the carpet although it was practically tingling to do just that.

My mother looked out the window as she recalled her story. "Well, I was born a rebel, refusing to come out into the world for a full three days." She shook her head. "My poor mother. I grew up in a religious household and when my parents both died I was passed on to the church elders to raise since I was only fifteen when they passed."

"I'm sorry," I offered, my gut twisting at the news of my grandparents that she'd never spoken about.

"No worries. It was a long time ago. But it was only then I realized that my parents were unique members of the church. In our house, we didn't have to lower our eyes and we could speak whenever we felt like we had something to say, but that wasn't the standard. Far from it. It was a severe way to grow up and I never embraced it."

Neither did I.

"Every day when I woke up I saw the light fading from my eyes as more and more rules were pushed down my throat. By the time they informed me that I was to be married to this man of the church. Richard was his name." She cringed. "I'd all but given up. I didn't know life outside the church and didn't think I could make it on my own. I had hoped that maybe Richard would be more like my parents. It only took meeting him a few times for me to realize he was perhaps the worst of them all. He treated me like a dog on the leash and always made sure the collar allowed me to breathe but always reminded me that just one pull in the wrong direction and I'd be choking."

I was crying inside for my mother but tried to remain impassive on the outside.

It wasn't easy.

"One weekend, my guardians brought me along to a

tent revival service to help. We stayed in a little motel and I'd go for walks around the town whenever I could sneak away for an hour or so. One day I saw a truck and camper for sale in a junkyard and something came over me. An idea I couldn't shake." My mother took up her knitting and placed it back down again.

She continued. "On the day I married Richard, I stole a gold crucifix that belonged to Richard and I brought it to the junkyard. I traded it and my wedding ring for the camper and the truck. I didn't make it far before the truck broke down on the side of the road. I got out and walked to find help and made sure to walk in the opposite direction of the fairgrounds because although the freedom I'd tasted was only a few miles from there I knew I'd never be going back. And that walk in the middle of the night all by myself? It was glorious. My first taste of actual freedom. The sounds of the swamp at night." She closed her eyes like she could still hear it. Then she inhaled deeply through her nose. "The smell of salty water and the sulfur." She opened her eyes again. "By the time I realized I was lost I didn't care if anyone ever found me ever again. I fell down an embankment and got stuck on this tiny strip of muddy land but it was too steep to climb my way back up to the top. As the water rose, I thought for sure that I was going to die there."

"What did you do?" I asked, leaning forward.

She shrugged and took up her knitting again. "There was nothing I could do. And there was something so...freeing about the experience that I sat down in the mud and I...I just started to laugh. And that's when Critter found me. Sitting in the mud, the water rising all around me when he zipped by on his little boat and did a double take. He stopped and pulled me out. I was covered in mosquito bites, mud from head to toe, and soaking wet and do you know what that man did?" she asked with a loving smile.

"No. What did he do?" I asked, leaning forward.

She smiled in a way that told me she couldn't believe it herself. "He started to laugh right along with me. The man had no idea why I was laughing but joined right on in. He took me back to his bar and while I cleaned up and changed my clothes he went and towed the truck and camper back to the bar. When I walked out all cleaned and mud free he looked up at me and I'll never forget what he said."

"What? What did he say?" I asked.

"He looked up and said, *it's you*. Like he'd been waiting for me his entire life." She looked out the window to where Critter was sitting on the porch, rocking in the chair, fiddling with something on his lap. "And then, before the coffee was ready in the morning, we'd fallen madly and deeply in love."

"That's a beautiful story," I said, and it really was. "What about this Richard guy?" I looked to the walls and to the floor then back again. Anywhere but at my mother. "Was...is he the father of your baby?"

My mother shook her head. "No, gosh no. I left before our wedding night took place. It luckily never got that far. This big baby girl right here," she patted her belly, "or at least I think she's a she, is one hundred percent Critter."

One hundred percent...Critter.

"You said you two are married? You and Critter I mean?"

"I sure am," she answered, humming and knitting once again. "The marriage to Richard was only a church ceremony. No paperwork so it wasn't legal in the eyes of the state. Luckily for me, the church abided by God's law, but not man's. Then, I was free to marry Critter."

She's legally married to Critter.

My mother looked as if she was about to say something but she stopped before the words came out. She turned her head from one side to the other like she was seeing me for the first time. There was a clarity in her eyes that wasn't there earlier, along with something else.

Recognition.

My stomach flipped. My heart hammered in my ears.

"Sawyer?" she asked in a whisper, blinking rapidly. "Is that you?"

"Yes, Mother. It's me," I said as gently as I could, keeping my expression as even as possible. I hadn't even realized I was crawling across the carpet toward her until I was kneeling before her, staring up into familiar loving eyes.

"My baby girl. It really is you," she said, dropping from the chair to her knees in front of me. She pulled me in for a hug and I couldn't stop the tears once they started and neither could my mother. We sat there, hugging and crying into each other's arms. "You're alive. He told me you were, but I didn't believe him. I needed to see you. You made it out. I'm sorry," she said into my hair, peppering kisses along my frizzy head. "I'm sorry for everything."

"I made it out, Mom. Because of you. Because of your letter and the box and your instructions. You sent me here. You got me out," I told her. As I spoke I felt some of the resentment I had been feeling toward her start to dissipate.

"I'm sorry I didn't tell you," she cried. "I couldn't. I needed to keep you safe. Forgive me sweet girl. I did what I thought was best but I made a mess of everything. I have so much to tell you," she said, sobbing against me. "There is more you need to know."

"You don't have to tell me all of it now," I replied against her shoulder as she squeezed me repeatedly as if she needed a constant reminder that I was really there as much as I needed one.

After a few moments, Mother's arms stiffened and before she pulled back I knew our time together had passed. When she looked me over again the glassiness in her eyes was back. "I better get off the floor. Critter doesn't want me to strain myself in my condition. Says it's not good for the baby." She stood up and sat back down on her chair, picking up her knitting once again. The half-dried tear stains on her cheeks were the only evidence of our stolen reunion.

I stood up to leave when Maddy came into the room and gave me a stern nod. "I should go. Thanks for having me, and thanks for telling me the story of how you met your husband."

She smiled at me sweetly. "That's no bother at all. I love telling that story. Half the people in this town are tired of it already. Thanks for coming to visit. Make sure to come by again," she said. "Maybe Sunday? On Sundays, I make my famous peach pie. It's Critter's favorite."

I wiped my wet face with the heel of my hand. "I'd like that very much if you're sure it's alright with you."

"Of course. I'd love that. See you Sunday," she said cheerily. "And don't worry about that adorable little boy of yours. Finn is welcome to come take sunflowers whenever he would like. We've got plenty."

Finn.

I gave her a small farewell wave then waited until I was down the hall almost to the front door before I whispered, "Bye, Mom." I didn't know how I'd feel seeing her that way, but as I watched her slip back into a place where I never existed I never expected for it to feel as if she had died all over again.

I RAN into Finn's arms the second I was back on the porch. I buried my face into the soft cotton of his t-shirt and didn't pull away until I heard Critter's voice.

"Sawyer?"

I turned around to face Critter who stood from his rocking chair with a knowing look etched in the lines of his face.

The face of my father.

We stood there, staring at one another for what felt like an eternity.

"Critter?" I asked as if I were seeing him for the first time.

He rocked forward slightly on the balls of his feet,

he folded his hands behind his back. For such a tall strong man my heart lurched at how vulnerable he appeared. "We heard you in there with her," Finn said from behind me.

Critter nodded. "You did good, kid. But if you don't mind, I'd...why is this so fucking hard," he grumbled. He took a deep breath. "I'd like for you to call me, Dad." His voice cracked on the last word.

My heart burst open, unleashing a powerful flood of emotions along with uncontrollable tears. I fell to my knees. Before I knew it, Critter had closed the distance between us and lifted me up off my knees, pulling me into his strong arms against his chest. He smelled like cigar smoke and cologne. That's what my dad smelled like and I'd remember it forever.

I was sobbing so hard it prevented me from speaking, but Critter watched me as I looked up and mouthed the words, "Hi, Dad."

He lifted me up, swaying me back and forth as my feet dangled off the porch. "Hey, kid." My tears soaked through his shirt as we squeezed each other tightly and he peppered kisses on the top of my head. "Welcome home, kiddo," he said on a choked sob. "Finally. Welcome fucking home."

We stayed that way for a long time, stuck together, reunited. Father and daughter.

And we cried.

We cried because we both finally knew the truth. We cried for the time lost between us. And although neither one of us said it out loud, I knew that somewhere in the time between those first tears falling and the sun sinking deep into the horizon, we were both crying for her.

———

THE SUN HAD JUST SETTLED down for the night. The star littered black sky had officially taken its turn guarding the earth.

Finn, Critter and I were still sitting on Critter's front porch. Critter and Finn were sipping beers. I settled for an iced tea after deciding that beer was an acquired taste, and I hadn't yet had the time to acquire it.

"Do you...do you need me to help take care of her?" I asked Critter. "My mother. It isn't fair for you to have to do it all alone."

He shook his head and took a sip of his beer. "Listen, kiddo, you've spent your entire life looking after your mother. You've done a good job. You did more than most would in your situation. Hell, you stayed when most would've cut bait and got out." He leaned forward on his elbows. "How about you step aside and let me do it for once? Besides, I've missed out on taking care of that woman for two decades. I've got a lot to make up for."

"I haven't asked you how you're holding up during all of this. So, how are you holding up?"

"I'm hanging in there. She's back but she's not completely back. It's going to take a little while to set her to rights again but I won't stop until my sunflower is back to one hundred percent."

"Are you the one who gave her this pendant?" I

asked, holding up the sunflower hanging from the chain on my neck.

"Yeah," he said, looking wistfully over to the sunflower field, back-lit by the newly risen moon. "I proposed to your mama in that field. We fell in love in that field. We...well, some things are better left unsaid."

I laughed and sipped my tea.

"There are things about my past you should know," Critter said. "Things I don't talk about openly. But you're my daughter and you should know these kinds of things about your old man. About who I am and what I've done in my past."

"Like what?" I asked hesitantly, chewing nervously on the inside of my cheek.

"I haven't always been the best model citizen of this town. I've done things. A lot of things. Some of them bad, real bad. Spent a few years in state prison back in my twenties."

"So, you fell into the bad crowd in your youth?" I suggested.

Critter shook his head and looked at me from over his beer bottle. "No, I was the person people fell into. I was the bad crowd or at least, I ran the bad crowd."

"Does my mother know?" I asked.

"Your mother knows everything about me." Critter chuckled. "Every ugly and dirty detail. And she loves me despite of it and sometimes because of it."

"If it didn't matter to her then it doesn't matter to me."

"I don't understand why she's like this now when she wasn't this way before," Finn chimed in.

Critter shook his head. "The shrink here thinks she's

49

been holding so much above her head and over the years the weight of it grew heavier and heavier. When we got her back here and she knew you were okay it was like her knees buckled and it finally all came crashing down around her."

"Do you think she'll ever be back to...normal? Whatever that might be?"

"Normal," Critter chuckled at the word. "And as for your mother, she's a force stronger than any damn hurricane I've ever encountered. She just needs a little rest. A little time. There is only so much one body and mind can process. She'll come back to us eventually. I'm certain of it."

"Can I ask you something?"

Critter nodded.

"She was gone for two decades. Why didn't you ever remarry or have kids?"

Critter sighed and looked to his hands for a moment before answering. "Because the kind of love your mother and I have is not the kind you can recover from. It's not a cold. It's not temporary. It's the kind that becomes a part of yourself. Like the blood in your veins. Getting over your mother just wasn't possible."

"You really do love her," I lamented.

"Yes, with everything I have and more. And you," Critter added, with watery eyes. "I can't make up for years of not being your dad, but I'd sure like to try, kiddo."

Kiddo. I loved every endearment Critter swung my way. They made me feel special.

Safe.

LOVED.

Richard had never called me anything other than Sawyer. Or *girl*. Like it was a bad word.

"I think I'd like that."

"You need to know that I never believed she left me willingly. Not once. You just don't up and walk away from what we had. Not possible. I looked for you two every damned day after she left me that note. Every fucking day. And, when I couldn't find you I thought you were dead."

"Why?"

"Because I never thought he'd let your mother or you live when he found out she was pregnant with you," Critter said, tightening his grip on his beer bottle.

"He probably would have," I agreed. "But as it turns out, I was the perfect leverage to hold over her head."

"I didn't know you were alive until a few months ago when this arrived," Critter reached into his back pocket and handed me an envelope with no return address. "I'll let her tell you what happened."

I took the letter from the envelope and although I knew she was inside the house I heard her voice in my head reading the letter to me as if she were still a ghost.

C-

I'm risking everything by sending this, but I must because I don't have much time left. It's too late for me, but it's not too late to save our daughter.

Help her before it's too late for her as well.

I love you. Always have. Always will.

Forever your sunflower,

-Caroline

Tears were streaming down my face. I looked from the letter back to Critter. "I still don't understand why she didn't stay. She could have fought him off or escaped and come back to you. Instead she stayed with him. For...over twenty years. Why?"

Critter held up his hand. "Richard threatened her with the death of her child. You. With killing me. He told her if she tried to escape he wouldn't stop until she watched us both die in front of her. I know what you might be thinking but your mother wasn't no coward. She did what she had to do and she stayed because she thought that was the best way to keep us both alive. She's not a coward. Not even close. That woman waded through the waters of hell with the devil himself to keep us safe." Critter shifted in his chair. He glanced up at the house.

"She's the bravest woman in the entire damned world."

Finn placed his hand on my shoulder and gave it a squeeze. I loved how he always seemed to know when I needed to be reassured and at that moment I needed it more than ever. I'd been wrong. My gut and my head and my heart had all thought the worst.

I'd been wrong.

So very very wrong.

"I never...wow," I said, instantly feeling hurt and shame at ever suggesting my mother was selfish.

"There are only two things I regret in this life. Not finding you two, getting to you sooner is one of those things."

"What's the other?" Finn asked, twirling his beer around in his hand.

Critter didn't hesitate when he glanced up at us with cold hatred in his eyes.

"Not killing that son of a bitch, Richard, twenty-two fuckin' years ago."

CHAPTER 6

FINN

W hen my phone rang, I left Sawyer and Critter on the porch to talk to answer it. "Hi, Mom."

"Honey, how are you? It's been days and you haven't called."

"I talked to you yesterday, Mom," I reminded her.

"Are you sure? It seems like longer."

"I'm sure," I said, smiling into the phone.

"You sound a lot different. Does this have anything to do with the girl I've heard all about from everyone in that town except my own son."

I looked to where Sawyer was talking with Critter and my heart warmed. "Yeah, something like that."

"Finn Hollis, you bring that girl up here for a visit the very second you get a chance. We'd come there, but your father's asthma has been acting up. It's a little too humid this time of year."

"Stop making me sound like an old man," my father grumbled in the background.

"Then stop doing old man things like sucking on your teeth after breakfast," my mother scolded.

"You two haven't changed," I said.

My mother's tone turned serious. "Finn, we haven't seen you in a long time. Well, not since…" she paused like she was waiting for something. A reaction of some sort.

"You can say her name, Mom. It's fine. Jackie. Her name was Jackie." I was downright proud of how far I'd come. Saying her name used to bring nothing but pain. Now it was a name associated with a girl I'd once loved and lost.

And that was okay.

She let out a sigh of relief. "Thank Christ himself. It wasn't long ago you treated her name like a swear word. A bad one. Like the one you called your English teacher in the third grade. What nine-year-old calls their teacher a cu—"

My father interrupted. "Son, are you coming up here or do we have to bribe you? We've only been asking for two years now," my dad yelled to the phone.

Phone calls with my parents used to be stressful. I'd spend every moment trying to convince them I was okay when I wasn't. Lately I hadn't even had the urge to hang up and throw my phone in the swamp.

I crossed my arms. "That depends. What have you got to bribe me with?"

"Cobbler and your favorite fried chicken sandwiches?" my mother asked. My stomach growled at the thought of my mother's famous chicken. "And I'll have Ethan come get you then you won't have to drive. And you'll bring that girl of yours so we can meet her?" she asked hopefully.

I looked to Sawyer and our eyes met. She smiled.

"Definitely."

CHAPTER 7

SAWYER

E ver since Critter and I spoke a few days before, I felt better. Lighter. But the lingering dread over an uncertain future was starting to weigh on me. I felt drained. My eyes were tired as was my mind. The thought that lingered with me the most, the one that whispered through my ears like an unseen mist was that Richard was still out there. There was a possibility he'd come for me. After all, I'd stolen from him and he hated me because he blamed me for my mother's death. Any other man in the world would have no reason to come find me, but Richard Dixon wasn't any other man. I knew sooner or later he'd come. I'd always known that. But one thing had changed.

Mom.

If Richard came for me and found her instead...I hated to think of what would happen. Maybe if we left Outskirts, just for a little while, just until the tent service packed up and left, then we could keep him from discovering she was alive.

I was about to voice the idea to Finn when he sat down beside me on the dock and distracted me with his bare chest and rippling muscles. When he smiled at me, my stomach and something a bit lower did a little flip of happiness.

"What's that look on your face? Not a good book?" he asked, pointing to the book open on my lap.

MODERN RELIGIONS FOR A MODERN WORLD

Book? What book?

He pointed again to my lap, smiling because he knew what kind of effect he had on me. "Oh. Yeah. This book. It's not that it's not good. It's that I don't think it's really what I was looking for," I said, staring down at the title of the chapter and reading it again in case I'd read it wrong the first time around.

Nope. I'd read it right.

"What?" Finn asked, leaning over to glance at what I'd been reading. I breathed in his fresh scent and leaned back into him ever so slightly to better feel the warmth of his chest through my thin tank top.

I scanned the article quickly and gave him the stand out points. "There is a religion called Church of the Flying Spaghetti Monster. The basis for it is that the followers of this religion believe a being they call the Flying Spaghetti Monster created the world and every-thing in it. It's literally flying pasta and meatballs," I said, pointing to the picture below the caption. I closed the book and set it to the side, shaking my head in disbelief.

"How is that any stranger than believing that a man walked on water or rose from the dead?" Finn asked, leaning back on his hands. "Or that cows are sacred animals? Or that there are people who keep a piece of toast for decades because they swear they can see Jesus Christ's image burned into it by the toaster."

"Well, now that you put it that way, Flying Spaghetti Monsters don't seem all that strange," I replied playfully.

Finn grabbed my hand. "That makes sense, but the thing is, this all may seem crazy to us but to a lot of people it brings them peace, makes them feel whole. Gives them purpose. It's not up to anyone to decide what's crazy and what's not. If it makes someone feel whole then more power to them."

"What religion did you grow up in?" I asked realizing I had no idea if Finn's family were people of faith or not.

Finn grimaced. "Uh, the kind that goes to church on Easter and Christmas but only if the parking lot wasn't too full and we didn't have to park in the mud across the street." He sat up and pushed my hair off my shoulder, tracing my collarbone with his finger. "What's really going on with the religious stuff, Say? You want to talk about it?"

I decided to go with the truth since anything else would sound even more strange. "I don't know what to believe anymore. It's scary not having a faith, but freeing at the same time. It's like I've got this chance to live my life on my own terms and by knowing all there is to know I won't feel like there is a small piece of me missing," I confessed. "I'm not a hundred percent sure, though. Maybe, I thought that if I read more—studied up on the religions of the world, then suddenly everything would make sense to me. But it doesn't. None of them actually make any sense to me at all."

"The people of those religions think they make perfect sense," he countered.

"Yes, that's the thing. They all have faith in what they believe and they all think they are right and they call it faith. I know about faith. The dictionary calls it confidence and belief in something based on spiritual apprehension rather than proof. But with all the religions out there in the world, some of them have to be wrong. Am I right? I mean, if there is one absolute then *most* of them have to be wrong."

Finn shrugged and rested his stubbly chin on my bare shoulder. "But what if they're all right?" He kissed the space between my neck and shoulder and I relaxed into his touch.

I smiled. "Then may the Spaghetti Monster bless us all."

Finn chuckled before his smile faded and his tone turned more serious. "Do you miss it? At least, parts of it? Your past, I mean?"

"No!" I said with a lot more force than I intended. "I mean, I felt like an outsider in the church because I was one. I couldn't fall in line and just blindly believe. And out here, as much as I love it, I still feel like an outsider. Every time Miller brings up a TV show or a reference to something I don't understand it's just a reminder that I didn't come from this world," I explained.

Finn remained quiet for a moment, staring at the ground.

"What?" I asked, wondering what was on his mind.

He blinked and looked back up at me. "Just had an idea…"

"And…"

He waved it off. "I'll tell you later. In the meantime, please don't base anything on Miller or what he says. He once called in sick to work to watch three days of a reality TV show about wives in Mississippi." He laced his fingers with mine. I loved how large his hand was compared to mine. His tanned against my pale.

"I just…I want to know things," I said. "Arm myself with knowledge. Figure out where it all came from and make my own decision about what I want to believe. If anything."

Finn nodded and there was another look on his face. Pride? "I think that's a great idea. Research it all and let me know when the Flying Pasta Monster service starts." He planted a quick kiss on my lips.

"Flying Spaghetti Monster," I corrected.

"That's so specific." Finn chuckled, pulling me up onto his lap.

"I was thinking of writing it all down in like a diary or journal. That way I can remember everything I learn and make notes."

"What about a blog?" Finn suggested.

"A blog?" I wrinkled my nose, unfamiliar with the term.

"Yeah, it's like writing to a diary or a journal except you post it online that way more people have access to it. They can learn from it as you learn from it. I think you'd be pretty great at it and I can help you put it together if you want."

"You'd do that? For me?" I asked, my heart fluttering and my skin warming under his touch.

"Don't you know by now?" Finn breathed, his gaze locked on mine. "I'd do anything for you."

My entire body shuddered against him as he pressed a kiss to my neck. Then, ever so slowly, he traced the outside of my ear with the tip of his tongue. Everything within me came alive. "What are you doing?" I asked, breathlessly.

"I'm helping," he insisted. "You want religion?" Finn pushed back a lock of my hair. "Then I'll get on my knees and worship you for the rest of my life. You want to save someone? You've already done it. You saved me. You want heaven?" His hand skated up the back of my skirt. I shivered. His deep voice hummed in my ear. "I'll take you there right now."

I ached for him to touch me. To give me more than just his delicious words. "Yes. Heaven. Please." I gasped as he hooked his fingers inside my panties and pulled them to the side.

"So wet for me," he groaned. He unbuckled his jeans and lifted his hips to push them down. He set me on my back making me brace myself on the edge of the dock. He didn't take his eyes off mine when he thrust inside of me, sending my spine arching off the dock as a bolt of pleasure shot through me.

"Fuck, that's so good. You're so good. Every time. Every fucking time," Finn groaned.

I pushed back against him as he took me quick and hard. It didn't take me long for the pleasure to burst inside of me. I saw stars. After a few furious strokes

Finn followed me over the edge and I relished the feeling of his hot release filling me.

We collapsed on top of the picture the Flying Spaghetti Monster. Finn rested his chest against my back without pulling out of my body.

"You know, I'm a sinner now. Probably even going to hell," I whispered, bringing his attention to the Bible my hand was still pressed against.

"That's not true," Finn argued, still trying to catch his breath.

"How can you be so sure?"

Finn rocked forward and I was instantly reminded he was still inside of me. "Because, you feel like heaven to me."

"TELL me more about how you grew up. Tell me how it was so different from here," Finn said as he traced lazy circles on my back and over the globes of my butt cheeks.

"You know most of it already," I said, turning to him. We were in his bed in the cabin after moving inside from the dock and quickly deciding we were nowhere near done with one another.

"Yes, but I want to know everything. What makes you YOU. Good or bad it made you who you are and I, for one, love who you are."

"You do?" I asked, although he'd already told me I never grew tired of hearing it. With Finn, I felt warm from the inside out. My entire being reacted to him from my nose to my toes. From my heart to my soul.

"I do. I love you. Fiercely. Possessively. Crazily. Always."

"That was beautiful."

"You're beautiful," he said, leaning in to kiss my shoulder. He continued to trace every little freckle and mole on my body.

"You know, if you keep tracing them all then we are going to be here for a while," I pointed out.

His dimple appeared with his smile. "I'm counting on it. Now. Talk."

I thought for a moment. I felt vulnerable opening up to him. I'd left out most of the details about my life although he knew the short version. It was almost as if I were keeping it to myself because it was my cross to bear and I didn't want to burden anyone else with it.

"I guess it was like living in a different universe. One where every day was the same. We didn't celebrate holidays or birthdays. I didn't understand if it was my house that was different because of my father's strictness and temper or if every family in the church was that way. Every day we lived the same lie over and over again. The lie that the church was about family. Family above all others. The most important thing in the world next to God himself. And who knows, maybe in other houses, in other families, they were different behind closed doors. Loving. Kind. Maybe they let the women eat at the same table or look them in the eye."

Finn's tracing paused then started again.

I continued. "Maybe their daughters were allowed to speak without having the man of the house's permission first. Maybe they didn't use physical force to discipline the poor dim-witted females whose only purpose in life was to have and raise the babies and serve their husbands."

I shuddered.

"That must have been rough."

"I grew numb to it after a while. It was the only life I knew. There were days that I'd sit in my room and feel guilty for wanting to leave. For wanting a different life. I thought it was selfish and that by not putting others before myself I was the biggest sinner of them all. And now I know how brave and selfless she was. Maybe I was the biggest sinner after all."

Finn laid down next to me facing sideways with his head on the pillow and his hand on my waist. "But you did put others before yourself. You stayed, didn't you? For your mom? She stayed for you and you stayed for her. She wasn't the only brave one. You were both brave. For one another."

"You think so?"

"Say, we're all selfish in some way. It's human nature. I'm selfish because I claimed you before you had a chance to experience this world and find someone better. Think about it this way. If I wasn't the selfish prick I am, we wouldn't even be together." He cupped my face in his hand. "But it doesn't matter. Because I'm never letting you go."

Finn climbed over me, trailing kisses down my body past my belly button then lower and lower still. The entire time between kisses and nips he repeated his earlier words.

"I love you. Fiercely. Possessively. Crazily. Always."

CHAPTER 8

SAWYER

"**D**on't go anywhere alone. Promise me," Finn said with his hand possessively draped over my leg. There was nothing about his demeanor to suggest he was joking and I had a feeling he wasn't going to let me out of the car until I agreed.

"I won't," I said, not wanting to make him worry. "I promise."

Finn leaned over to me and pressed a kiss to my temple. "Thank you."

I blushed. "I'm going upstairs to Josh's apartment and then she is going to take me to the library." I got out of the car and shut the door.

"I'll pick you up. That gives me time to get everything ready for our trip," Finn said, casually tossing out the idea I'd never heard him speak of before while backing up the car.

"What trip?" I called out over the sound of his roaring engine and the tires rolling over rock and gravel.

"What?" he yelled back, cupping his ear and smiling from ear to ear. "I can't hear you?"

"What trip?" I yelled louder.

He put the truck in drive and flashed me a wink before taking off.

"OH SHIT," Josh called out, I spun to find her leaning over the third story balcony of her apartment building. I figured she was there because Finn wouldn't have driven off otherwise. "Sounds like Finn's up to no good."

It had been a few days since I last spoke to Josh. Although Finn had filled her in on all that was going on, I felt like there was a gap in my life that needed to be filled by a few minutes in her company.

"Why is your face doing that weird thing where you don't blink. Are your eyeballs gonna fall out? 'Cause a warning would be nice. Or...shit. Are you gonna have a stroke because I don't think my renter's insurance covers that, so if you are I recommend stepping outside of the building first," Josh said playfully even though her look of concern was genuine. She opened the door and stepped aside to let me in. I handed her the bag containing the soup from the bakery she'd asked me to pick up on the way.

"I don't think so?" I said but it came out as a question. I set my bag down on her counter and

"With all the shit you've had going on? I wouldn't be surprised. How you holding up?"

"I'm...okay. It's hard to be happy about my mom

being alive and Critter being my dad when I don't know if my mom is going to be okay yet and if the threat of Richard is still out there," I said, staring down at the counter. "It will always be out there."

"Not always. We're gonna put our heads together and think of something. I'm going to spin my wheels until the rubber falls off thinking of any way I can help." She pushed my chin up with her hand. "Now chin-up, buttercup."

Josh came over and embraced me in a tight hug. She smelled like coconut lotion and her skin was warm like she'd been sitting outside. "I'm here if you need me. Always," she reminded me, searching my eyes for understanding.

I nodded and looked away before the tears came. I'd had enough of those for quite some time and I knew that once I opened the faucet it would be hard to shut it down again.

"What is this about Finn taking you on a trip tonight?" Josh asked.

"You know about as much as I do. Nothing."

"Typical Finn," Josh said with a roll of her eyes. She took the soup out of the bag and set it on the counter, carefully taking off the lid to release the steam. She opened a drawer and retrieved a spoon.

"Who is that for, anyway?" I asked.

Josh pointed a finger at the closed bedroom door and motioned for me to follow her inside.

Something under the covers on her bed moved and it took me a moment to realize it there was a dark head of hair sticking out from the top of the stack of white fluffy pillows. Not just any head.

Miller's head.

"I'm soooooo sick," he moaned, rolling over with the blanket bunched up in his fists, pulling it up over his head.

Josh leaned over him and shouted through the covers. "The only thing you have is a case of the man-flu! It's not deadly, just annoying as all hell." She looked over at me. "Especially to the female population."

Miller pulled the blanket back down revealing a slightly reddened nose. He sniffled. "Don't yell at me. I don't feel well. I think it's the black plague." He lowered his voice to a whispery rasp. "Who knows how much time I have left..." he said, followed by a dramatic series of coughs into his closed fist.

"Here is your damn chicken soup," Josh barked and plopped the bowl down onto the nightstand, sloshing some over the side.

"Stars or noodles?" Miller asked without so much as glancing at the bowl or what was inside. He pulled the covers back up over his nose, peeking out at Josh over the top.

Josh rolled her eyes and placed a hand on her jutted hip. "At this rate, just be grateful it's not arsenic." She turned and ushered me from the room.

"It's too far away," Miller whined, making a grabby motion with his hand for the soup which was in arm's reach if he would've actually tried to reach it. "I can't...I can't reach iiiiiiit. Don't leave me like this, woman!"

"He doesn't even have a fever," Josh informed me, ignoring Miller and shutting the door.

"Sawyer, why are you letting her be so cruellll!!!!"

Josh sneezed into her elbow and retrieved a tissue

from the box off the counter to briefly blow her nose. "I have the same exact cold," she said, pitching the tissue into the trash and washing her hands in the kitchen sink. "And see how differently we're handling it?"

"Just a little different," I agreed.

She stared at the closed door. "He needs to woman-the-hell-up because I swear to God if he asks for one more thing I'm gonna load him in the truck and toss him in the drunk tank. He can sleep it off like Mr. Ward has to every time the Panthers lose and he drowns his sorrows in his grandfather's moonshine."

"You wouldn't!" Miller shouted came from the other side of the door.

"Oh yeah? Try me!" She shouted back.

After a few seconds, when no reply came, she turned to me. "I'm sorry about that. Are you alright? I mean, are you REALLY alright? I feel like we haven't had a ton of time to talk and I've been busy dealing with Mr. Crazy Possessive in there."

Fiercely. Possessively. Crazily.

"Josh, can I ask you something? You don't have to answer but I'm curious."

"Miller asked me to use my nail to reach something in his nose he couldn't. I told him if he asked me again I'd kick him in the dick, but the point is that no question besides that one, will offend me at this point."

"Gross, and noted. I'm curious," I pointed to the bedroom, "do you love him?"

Josh narrowed her eyes to slits. "Today might not be the best day to ask me that."

Josh and Miller were complete opposites. , you'd think they hated each other. But once I discovered they were an item, and had been for a long time, I saw it. The love they didn't want anyone else to see. I can look back on all our interactions and pick up on the exchange of glances. The way Miller knew where she was in the room at all times. The way they always seem to be touching one another when they thought no one was paying attention. It was so glaringly obvious now that I don't know how I ever missed it to begin with.

"The last time I saw you two you were at each other's throats. Have you two talked things out?" I asked, sipping from the bottle of water she handed me from the fridge.

Josh shook her head. "Only if you consider him showing up at my door, sneezing in my face and telling me he loves me and needs me to take care of him before falling face first into my bed, talking things out then, yeah. I guess we talked."

"The last time I saw you was the first time I'd seen you really angry at him. Not playfully angry but truly angry."

Josh strolled over to the couch and plopped down, tucking one foot underneath of her. I took a seat on the opposite end and mirrored her position.

"Yeah, that," she said, pinching her bottom lip and shaking her head, she stared blankly at the wall. "I still don't really know what that was. When it comes to Miller I think that I try to push back all the feelings so much that when they push through they spring out like a damn jack-in-the-box."

"Maybe talking to him about it will help," I suggested, although I wasn't one to give advice. I'd only had one romantic relationship and I was guessing as I went.

"You know?" Josh asked, narrowing her eyes, "for someone who claims to be innocent when it comes to a lot of things you sure can Dr. Phil a situation like a champion."

I didn't know who Dr. Phil was, but the way Josh said it made it sound like a good thing.

"Or maybe," she nudged my arm, "you're just a really good friend."

My chest swelled. "Before I came here I never had a real friend. You're officially my first one. And thank you. For listening. For everything. I don't know what I'd do without you."

Either Josh wasn't surprised or she hid it well. "And don't forget you've also got Miss Miller in there." She jerked her thumb to the room. "We're more than friends though, Say. We're family."

Family.

When I first arrived in The Outskirts I didn't have anyone, and now it seemed that I was adding to my family daily.

"I'm sorry. I know this has all got to be hard with your mother and all," Josh said, taking my hand in hers and giving it a squeeze. "Do you want to talk about it?"

"No. I had a good talk with my mother when she was with it for a bit and then Critter and then Finn. I think I'm all talked out for now."

And all cried out. And emotionally exhausted.

"Good because after dealing with Miss Prissy Pants I could use some damn silence," Josh argued.

"I heard that!" Miller called out. "Save me, Sawyer. She's sooooo mean."

"These walls are too damn thin," Josh said. She squeezed my hand. "Well, you know that I'm here for you, Sawyer. No matter what you need. I'm here. Finn too."

All I could do was nod in response. Josh was really a great friend and I was truly lucky to have her. I made a move to stand up when I heard Finn's truck pull into the parking lot but swayed and sat back down when I suddenly felt dizzy.

"You okay?" Josh asked. She pressed the back of her hand to my head then felt my pulse in my neck. "No fever. Pulse is a little quick."

"I'm fine. I think I stood up too fast or maybe I'm just getting the same cold you and Miller have."

She moved her fingers around my throat pressing up and down in various spots. "No swollen glands either. Answer me this, do you have the urge to complain about simple sneezing and coughing? Do you feel the need to be coddled while whining incessantly for no reason whatsoever?"

I shook my head. "No. None of that."

Josh looked to the bedroom door and grumbled. "Then you definitely don't have what Miller has."

"I heard that too!"

Josh ignored him. "Anyways, where do you think Finn is taking you?"

I racked my brain. "I have no idea at all."

"I can't wait to find out where. Call and tell me as soon as you know. Don't you just love surprises?" Josh bounced on the cushion excitedly.

I loved that Finn was planning a trip for us, but I came from a place where surprises ended in black eyes, bruises, and bleeding. So no, in all honesty I couldn't say that I liked surprises.

Not at all.

Especially, the kind we never saw coming.

CHAPTER 9

FINN

As the small twin-engine plane ascended the look on Sawyer's face was one I will remember for the rest of my life. She paled as we gained altitude and her head stayed plastered to the back of her seat.

"Are you going to be okay?" I asked.

"I've never been on a plane before," she said, her voice a much higher pitch than usual.

Ethan, my parent's neighbor, who they've known for the last three years, turned around from the front seat of the plane. He took one look at Sawyer's face and said, "First time on a plane?"

"How did you know?" she asked shakily. Her hand squeezed mine tighter and tighter with each bump and jolt of the plane. I didn't even care that I was losing circulation. I was too excited that I got to share in Sawyer's first plane ride with her.

"Just a guess," Ethan said with a smile. "You are doing great!" He turned back around to the controls.

We entered a puffy white cloud. The plane began to shake like a bus driving over a rocky road.

"Is this normal?" she asked. Her knee bounced furiously until I placed my hand over it before she bounced herself right out of the plane.

"You are doing great, baby," I reassured her. "And yes, this is all normal."

"Do you remember when you told me all of those facts during the storm to distract me?"

"Of course," I said. How could I ever forget? It was one of the best nights of my life. It was the first time I held Sawyer in my arms. In my bed.

"Do you have any more of those? I could really use them right now." The plane dipped to the left. A smooth turn. Sawyer jumped as if someone had scared her from behind.

I lost all feeling in my hand. I still didn't care. "Did you know, that in the history of aviation, that turbulence has never taken down a plane before?"

She shook her head in response squeezing her eyes shut.

"it's true. Turbulence is perfectly normal. It's not an indication of engine trouble. Think of it like a car on a bumpy road. These planes were made to drive on bumpy roads. Or bumpy air, I should say."

The plane leveled off. Sawyer grabbed her midsection.

"Are you going to be sick?" I asked.

Sawyer shook her head furiously from side to side.

The bumps subsided. The ride became smooth. "Look," I told Sawyer, "open your eyes."

"No!" she exclaimed, placing her hands over her already closed eyes.

"Do you feel it? No more bumps. It's beautiful down there. You need to see it." When that didn't work, I tried another tactic. "Where is my brave girl? Where is the one who wouldn't let anything stop her. Who was fearless when she should've been afraid? I need that girl to open her eyes and look because I know she would be upset when she found out what she missed. Because right now from where I'm sitting the view is incredible."

I lightly tugged on Sawyer's wrist, removing her hand from her eyes. Slowly and reluctantly she opened her eyes and squinted from the sun. Once her eyes adjusted, I leaned over her toward the window forcing her closer so she could see the ground below. "Isn't it amazing?"

Sawyer only nodded. Her lips parted. Wonder replaced the fear in her eyes. Her knee stopped bouncing. Her hand released mine as she pressed it to the window, trying to get a better glimpse of the earth beneath us. "It's sooo. Wow."

For the rest of the flight, Sawyer could not peel her eyes from the window. Right before we landed, she turned to me and said, "It makes you think, doesn't it?"

"About what?"

"About how unimportant it all is. And at the same time how important it all is."

I didn't know exactly what she was trying to say. All I knew was up most important thing in the world to me was sitting right next to me, squealing with joy as the wheels hit the tarmac.

CHAPTER 10

SAWYER

"Where are we exactly?" I asked as Ethan dropped us off in the driveway of a cabin-style home built into the side of a mountain.

Finn thanked Ethan who pointed to his own home across the narrow path. "That's me if you need anything."

Ethan backed up and pulled into his own driveway.

"We are in the Georgia mountains."

"Whose house is this?" I asked, just as an excited scream pierced the night air.

"My baby is home!"

The front door flung open and a tiny woman leapt down the porch, running toward Finn with open arms and colliding into him with such force it knocked him back a step.

"Hey, Mom. Good to see you too," Finn chuckled against her head, returning her hug.

Mother.

We are at his parents' house.

I began to panic more than I had on the plane. My palms grew sweaty. My throat went dry. At least the flight he'd told me about a few hours beforehand. He'd given me no warning at all about this.

Finn's mother pulled back but kept her hands on his arms. "Let me look at you," she said, giving her son a once over. Her eyes were dark brown and full of warmth. Her short hair was a light strawberry blonde. She looked nothing like Finn at all and was at least a foot shorter than him. "You look great, honey." Her eyes welled up with happy tears.

"None of that now, Ma. But you look great too," Finn said. He placed an arm around my shoulder and pulled me into him. "Mom, this is…"

"This is the one!" his mom shrieked, pulling me into her embrace. "It's so wonderful to finally meet you. You are absolutely stunning. Finn, you didn't tell me she was this beautiful." She whispered her next words in my ear. "Thank you."

When I pulled back to ask her why she was thanking me, I realized I'd been wrong. She did have one resemblance to Finn. The dimple that popped out on her cheek when she smiled.

"Are y'all gonna stand out there and hug all day or you gonna come on in?" Another loud yet much deeper voice boomed from the door.

Finn and his mother walked me up to the front steps to meet the man who was Finn, just older. White hair where Finn's was dirty blonde. A few more lines on his slightly reddened face. But his height, build, and even the way he was standing with his arms crossed over his chest was entirely Finn.

"It's eerie isn't it, darling?" Finn's mom whispered when she saw me staring between the two men.

I could only nod. I didn't know if eerie was the right word, but it was certainly interesting how it appeared that the mold used to make Finn's father was reused to make Finn.

"Nice seeing you again, son," Finn's dad said. "Been too damn long." He held out his hand but the second Finn placed his hand out his father took it and pulled him in for a one-armed hug. "Get over here."

"Great seeing you again too, old man," Finn said sounding genuine. I couldn't help but smile. His happiness was downright infectious.

"Old man? I don't look a day over fifty-two," his dad argued, puffing out his chest.

"That's because you ARE fifty-two," Finn's mother said with a playful shove to his shoulder.

"This must be Sawyer," his dad said, turning his attention and his Finn-like killer smile on me.

I couldn't help but smile back. "It's great meeting you both, Mr. and Mrs. Hollis. Thank you for having me in your home." I instantly realized we were still on the porch. "Or…outside of your home?" I amended.

Finn placed a hand on the small of my back. A reassuring gesture I desperately needed. I don't know why I was suddenly nervous to meet new people. I'd been doing it practically every single day for months.

But this is your first time meeting the parents of the man you love.

"No need for the formalities, darling," Mr. Hollis chuckled. "You can call me Joe and this here beautiful lady is my Josie."

"Joe and Josie?" I raised my eyebrows at the similar yet adorably fitting names.

Josie placed an arm around my shoulder, pulling me away from Finn and leading me into the house. Joe and Finn followed closely behind. "You think that's weird?" she whispered. "You should meet our neighbors. Sam and Samantha."

I chuckled.

"Although I think these kids here got us beat with the cute names, hun," Joe chimed in.

"How is that..." Finn's mom trailed off. She stopped walking and spun around as the realization hit her.

"I knew you'd get a kick out of it," Finn said with a proud smile. "Since it is your favorite book and all."

Josie clapped her hands together and looked like she was about to melt into the wood floor. She glanced between us with a smile that took up her entire face.

"Finn and Sawyer!"

CHAPTER 11

FINN

We ate my mother's famous roast chicken for dinner. It tasted better than I remembered. The conversation was light and filled with laughter. I found myself reaching over several times to squeeze Sawyer's hand or rub my foot against her calf under the table to reassure her. Although after a while it was clear her nerves had faded and she was just another Hollis sitting around the dinner table.

Just another Hollis.

Something about that made me want to sweep her off to a cave somewhere. I doubted the twin bed in my old bedroom would be as manly, it was going to have to do.

My caveman urges were going to have to wait. After dinner, my father and I sat out on the back deck while my mother insisted that Sawyer stay in to help her with her famous cobbler.

"Since when does Mom need help with dessert?" I asked, taking the cigar my father handed to me and biting off the end to light it. Cigars weren't really my thing but it was almost a tradition that every time I'd visited we'd smoke one and shoot the shit.

"She don't. That woman can bake with her eyes shut and her hands tied behind her back." He held up the cigar in his hand. "It's been too long since we had one of these," he said, lighting his cigar and puffing on it until the tip turned red then handing it to me to do the same. I took a puff and blew it out.

"Yeah, Dad," I agreed. "Way too long."

"You better now, kid? 'Cause, you look better than the last time I saw you when you practically tossed your mama and I out on our asses when we came to check on ya after Jackie passed. I know you told us that you were fine even when you wasn't even close to fine. Broke our hearts when we realized there wasn't nothing we could do for you but let you work it out on your own. And I know it was hard, but I'm glad you continued taking your mama's calls. It meant the world to her to know you were still trudging through the mess you made of your life instead of giving up on it."

I hated being responsible for their pain while I was going through mine. "I'm sorry," I said. "I really am. Couldn't see past my own shi…" my father glared at me. I chuckled. "stuff, to understand what I was putting you through."

My chest tightened at the thought of my parents suffering because of me.

"Yes, you hurt us. But yes, you are very forgiven. Always," my dad said, patting the top of my hand.

"Beat around the bush why don't ya," I said playfully.

My dad scoffed. "Life's too short to beat around it when you can carve your way through it in half the time and sit back with a beer and a cigar for the other half."

"There was nothing you guys could've done to help me see my way clear of my own bullshit back then. But, yeah. I'm better now. I'm sorry I put you through all that."

Dad looked down at his cigar, turning it around in his fingers like it somehow held all the answers. "Looks like Sawyer may have played a part in getting you back to us." He gestured to the window where Mom was talking enthusiastically, waving a rolling pin around in her hand while Sawyer laughed at whatever embarrassing story she was probably telling about my childhood. It meant everything to me to have her there. To be part of my family. The three people I cared about most in the world were under one roof and it was a kind of feeling of being complete that I never thought I'd ever have.

He couldn't have been more right. "She was the first person to come along who made me miss living. I wasn't expecting her. Or the way she made me feel. Took me by complete surprise."

"The good ones always do." Dad nodded like he understood exactly what I was saying although I didn't quite understand it myself. "I see the way you look at that girl. That's what I like to call the forever factor. I had it in my eyes when I saw your mother for the first time." He blew out a breath like he couldn't believe it himself. He glanced back through the window.

"You still have it when you look at her now," I said.

"That's what FOREVER means, son."

I laughed and took another puff of my cigar. Forever was exactly what I wanted with Sawyer. But I'd already taken so much from her. How could I ask her for forever right now when she's experienced so little out of life?

"Does Sawyer know how you feel? How deep this runs for you?" he asked, like he was reading my mind.

I shrugged. "I think so, but her life's...complicated. This is all new for her." I looked up at the sky. "New for me too."

"I can see that. You never looked at Jackie that way. She was a good kid and all. I miss her like she was my own daughter, but she wasn't your forever factor."

"No, she wasn't." I waited for the familiar sting of guilt to follow those words, but it never came.

"So, you don't want to scare Sawyer off with the enormity of your feelings. Then tell me, son, how's your woo?"

"My what?" I asked, choking on the smoke. I reached down to the beer on the deck next to my chair and took a healthy gulp.

My father cocked an eyebrow and gave me a side glare that was so heated it could melt metal. He shifted toward me in his seat. "You're a Hollis, son. Please tell me that you've been wooing the girl and not just practicing marital relations. Tell me you know how to woo."

"You do have a way with words," I chuckled. Also, he had a point.

Dad rolled his eyes. "You want to lock her down on forever but you're not wooing her? Have you even taken her out on a proper date?"

"I...shit," I said, leaning back and taking another puff on my cigar. "No. No, I haven't."

My dad scoffed. "You best get to it. If you don't want to dump your load of feelings on your forever girl without scaring the bees out of the hive then you, son, are gonna have to woo her first." Dad blew out a perfect smoke ring.

I glanced back to the house. My eyes met Sawyer's briefly met through the window. She blushed and went back to listening to whatever story my mom was telling.

I loved that blush. I loved that her entire body turned pink when she was turned on.

I didn't love that my dad was right.

"I hate it when you're right," I grumbled, not imagining how I'd been so naive. Between rejoining society and all the shit going down with Sawyer's parents, I'd skipped right over dating her.

I felt a blunt slap on the back of my head. I turned to find my father setting a rolled-up newspaper down on the deck. "What the hell was that for?"

"She's never been on a date before, right?" he asked. "You've taken up with her. Practically living together and you ain't took her on one single date." My dad rolled his eyes and whistled through his disappointment. "Not a movie not a dinner. Nothing. You even my son or should I get one of them fancy DNA tests of the internets?"

"Shit," I muttered, wiping my hand down my face and scratching the stubble on my chin.

"In case you were still wondering," my dad said. "That slap was for picking the apple before it had time to fall from the tree. Raised you better than that, son."

"Yeah, you did," I agreed.

My father turned his face upward and looked to the stars, reclining in his creaky lawn chair. I did the same.

"Whose side are you on anyway?" I asked after a few moments of silence.

Dad chuckled and I knew exactly what he was going to say because it was how he always answered the question whenever I talked to him in the past about my mother or even Jackie.

"Hers, son. Always hers."

FINN

I'd been a selfish prick.

Which was fitting because when it came to Sawyer it seems that it's also what I'd been thinking with instead of my brain. My father was right. I'd put the apple before the falling tree or whatever garbled mumbo jumbo he said that broke through to me.

She's never been on a date.

I'd been inside of her and never taken her on a date. Sure, I'd slept with plenty of women I'd never actually dated before, but Sawyer was unlike anyone I'd ever met, which was why the date I had planned was far from traditional.

With everything that's been going on, I hadn't realized we'd completely skipped a step. Actually, we'd skipped several steps. We went from the occasional kiss to keep her from freaking out to having her in my bed every night. I was over the moon happy but I hadn't stopped for one single second to think about all the things she's never experienced. All the things she's missed out on.

Sawyer had never so much as experienced high school or prom or a football game and at the first possible moment, I'd claimed her as mine and somewhere in all the beautiful chaos of falling for her I'd forgotten to date her.

I did deserve that slap my dad had given me.

I needed another one when every impure thought known to man crossed my mind as Sawyer stepped out of the bedroom wearing a white sundress that hugged her every curve.

"Did you get a haircut?" Sawyer asked as she met me on my parents' front porch. She smelled like lavender and vanilla. My favorite scent since I'd come to know her and one I now uniquely identified with all things Sawyer.

I made a note to thank my mother for taking Sawyer shopping in town today. Her dress was the kind that tied behind her neck and put her fantastic tits on display with just a hint of cleavage. I was already flexing my fingers to keep myself from untying it and letting it fall open. It hugged her small waist and perky ass then flared out just enough to gently swish against where the material stopped on the middle of her thigh.

I swallowed hard.

Sawyer nervously tucked one side of her auburn hair behind her ear, shuffling under the scrutiny of my gaze as I took in the magnificent creature before me.

"You are stunning," I finally managed to say. Clearing my throat and trying to get my head back in the game. She blushed under her freckles and I coughed because my heart literally skipped a beat. "The most beautiful thing I'd ever laid eyes on."

"You know. When we first met you used to be kind of..."

"Mean?"

She shook her head. "No, what's the word Josh would use?" she snapped. "An asshole. You were such an asshole."

I bent over with laughter. "Is it wrong that I find you swearing to be hilarious, adorable, and a complete turn-on?"

"I think that's acceptable." She looked up at me from under her long black lashes. "Thank you. And...your hair? Did you get it cut?" Sawyer pressed her beautiful pink lips together.

I couldn't believe this girl was mine.

"Finn?" she asked, dragging me to the present.

"Oh. Yeah. My hair. My mom gave me a trim. Said I looked like I crawled out of the swamp, not live beside it." I patted the top of my head like a dancing monkey in a circus sideshow. "She was right. It needed it. It had been a while." I'd always been confident in my looks and I loved the way Sawyer looked at and appreciated my body, but this was the first time in my life I was seeking approval from a girl. It was like I needed her to think I was good enough for her.

I wasn't. Never would be.

But still, I wanted her to think it.

It was then I realized how nervous I was. Which was stupid because we were practically living together. But this was different. Deeper somehow. More meaningful.

"It looks really great," she said, appraising my short-sleeved button-down shirt that hugged my biceps, fitted dark jeans and black boots. "YOU look really great." That fucking blush, the way the color on her cheeks matched her full lips. It made me ache to touch her, but I told myself I was going to behave. She deserved this night and so much more.

That didn't mean it wasn't going to be a long night.

"You really don't know how fucking sexy you are," I said. I'd drastically cut down on the smokes but I light a cigarette mostly so that I wouldn't throw her down and the deck and make her scream loud enough to wake my parents— who'd fallen asleep in the living room watching Jeopardy over an hour before the sun had even set.

"You sure do have a way with words, Finn Hollis." Her golden eyes were bright with questions and wonderment. Her pupils wild and wide. "Are you sure you're the same man I met in the clearing?"

"No. I'm not the same," I admitted. "Not since you."

She stared at me like she was stunned by my words until I took a drag of my cigarette and she blinked rapidly. "So, where exactly are you taking me?"

"It's…a surprise." I blew out the smoke and stubbed out my cigarette. I grabbed her by the waist and pulled her against me. Inhaling her scent.

Just a little bit of her to hold me over.

"Did you just smell me?" she asked with a nervous laugh.

"I sure fucking did." There was no point in denying it.

"So, how do I smell?"

"Delicious," I groaned. "Always delicious."

95

During the entire ride in my dad's truck, I was trying to casually adjust my hard-on. I felt like a thirteen-year-old who could barely control himself. I'd never been that way before but I found it impossible not to think about what was going on in my pants when everything Sawyer did seemed to send a jolt right between my legs. Like when I noticed her dress had ridden up on her thighs. When she crossed and uncrossed her legs and I caught a glimpse of white cotton between her legs. When she ran the tip of her index finger over the light sheen of gloss on her plump lower lip in the rearview mirror.

Yep. Long fucking night.

You'd think that once I'd had Sawyer that the desire for her would dwindle, like it had in the past with every other girl I'd been with, but that wasn't the case at all. It was like every time Sawyer was around me I was more and more infected by this disease of need.

A disease I never wanted to be cured of.

A disease I'd gladly die from while thanking the universe for bestowing it upon me with my last damned breath.

"Are you okay?" Sawyer asked, resting her hand on my thigh and giving me a gentle squeeze.

I stifled a groan. "Never better," I choked out.

"You look like you have something on your mind."

"Me? Nah. Not a damned thing." I pulled into the empty field beside the mountain and turned the engine to idle.

"Are you sure? We can do this another time if you don't—"

"No," I snapped. "You really want to know what I'm thinking about?" I asked with a laugh.

"Yes. Of course," she asked innocently, having no clue how much she affected me. "Okay, the entire ride here I was thinking of how much of you I still haven't explored. About how I'd like to trace my tongue over every single sexy freckled inch of you. About the way you blush before I make you come. About how you pull my hair when I'm kissing you between you—"

"Ooohh," she squealed, placing a hand over her mouth. There was that blush again. Her nipples peaked behind the fabric of her dress.

"But I'm trying to be a gentleman over here before my father kicks my ass for not taking you on a proper date."

"That's what this is all about?" she asked, sliding over to kiss me on the cheek.

I closed my eyes to collect myself and when I opened them back up I trained my eyes on hers. "Yes. If you don't mind, would you please stop being so incredibly sexy so I can do this properly?"

She leaned back in her seat and pressed her lips together. "," she said. "Where are we going anyway?" she asked, looking around at our dark surroundings.

I rounded the truck and helped her down, grabbing the backpack and picnic basket from the backseat I'd thrown in earlier with a little packing help from Mom.

"We are going right here," I said, laying out the blanket on the ground. "Sit." She sat and waited while I gathered the rest of what I needed. I set up the portable projector on the hood of the truck, pointing it toward the side of the mountain. I grabbed the remote and joined her on the blanket, pulling another one from the bag in case she got cold.

"There isn't a ton of date options in The Outskirts, same goes for the mountains. I did some research and the nearest movie theater to my parents' place isn't all that near. An hour's drive and it's playing something I think I saw in high school."

"I like this better," Sawyer said. "It's more...us."

"You haven't seen anything yet." I set out the food and snacks on the blanket and passed her a bag of popcorn. I made sure I was watching her face and not the side of the mountain which lit up when I pressed play on the remote.

"Wow," she exclaimed, craning her neck to the twenty-foot movie screen now projected on top of the rock in front of us. "What is this?"

"This is dinner and a movie," I explained, popping a piece of her popcorn in my mouth.

"This is really nice," she said, shoving a handful of popcorn in her mouth. "And this is sooooo good." She spoke with her mouth full and when popcorn shot from her mouth she laughed around her full chipmunk cheeks.

I was just about to press play when Sawyer said something that made me pause. "I loved meeting your parents. Thank you so much for bringing me here. It was everything I thought it was supposed to be."

"Everything you thought what could be?"

She sighed as if she were content. "Family."

I always knew my parents were great. They'd put up with a lot of shit in my earlier years and even more shit as I got older. But suddenly I was seeing them from

Sawyer's eyes. "You know, I didn't even think about how this could possibly upset you. I'm sorry."

She shook her head. "No. It was wonderful. They were so kind and gracious. They laughed and smiled and laughed some more when I spilled the water all over the table." She chuckled as I kissed her head. "They were amazing."

"They are pretty great. And they loved you."

"Because you love me," she said, like she was finally getting it.

I shook my head. "No, because YOU are amazing."

I pressed play on the remote before I completely forgot about everything except stripping Sawyer naked and fucking her in the middle of the damn field. Music started playing from the speaker attached to the projector. Sawyer's eyes lit up as she followed the stream of light over our heads to the wide tree in front of us where the opening credits of the movie were rolling.

"What movie is this?" she asked, bouncing on her butt and clapping her hands together. "What's it about?"

"There were only a handful of movies that worked with this projector in my parents' basement. One was about sharks, another about war, a documentary made in the seventies about porn."

"What's porn?"

"Uh...well." I felt my own face growing hot.

Sawyer remained expressionless while I stumbled around an explanation until she broke out into a fit of laughter. "Just kidding. I know what it is. But I loved that you're the one blushing now."

I reached in and tossed some popcorn at her hair which she expertly dodged.

"*Anyway*, to answer your earlier question. This one is called Juno. It's supposed to be a comedy. Other than that, I don't know much about it."

"I'm sure I'll love it," she said, her wide smile beaming in the dark almost as bright as the light on the projector.

"Come here," I said, pulling Sawyer into the crook of my arm. She snuggled against me while we snacked and watched the movie which wasn't as funny as I thought it would be considering it turned out to be about teen pregnancy and giving a baby up for adoption. Spoiler alert: it ended with both the teenage mother and father crying in a hospital room over the loss of their baby.

As the closing credits rolled, I looked over to Sawyer who had a confused look on her face. "What's wrong?" I asked.

She lifted her head to look at me. "Nothing, this was just...this was everything, Finn. I'm happy. YOU make me happy. Thank you." She placed her head back on my chest and I could feel her breath against my skin through the slit between the button of my shirt. She kissed my chest through the fabric.

"Can you..." she started, but then stopped. "I mean, can we..."

"Sawyer, all you need to do is ask and it's yours. I've told you that," I said, feeling the heat of her skin through our clothes.

She fiddled with the buttons of my shirt. I reached

down between her fingers and slipped the button out of the hole. "Is that what you wanted?" I asked on a rasp.

She nodded.

"Tell me," I whispered. "Tell me what you want."

She looked up at me. Her golden eyes dark. Her pupils large and glistening. "I want *you*."

"Thank, Christ," I swore, pushing her over onto her back and removing my shirt in record time. I pressed my lips to hers. She opened immediately so our tongues could meet and dance together. We groaned and moaned into one another as she reached for my belt buckle. When she had it through the loops, I popped the button and reached under her dress, pulling those white teasing panties down her legs. She used her feet to push down my jeans past my hips. My hard cock sprang free and I moaned when the tip pressed against the heat from her core. I stroked myself up and down against her pussy, coating my cock in her wetness. Teasing us both.

"Inside me, please," she rasped, rocking against me, lifting her hips to feel more of me.

"Finally," I ground out, thrusting my hips forward and pushing into her in one long hard thrust. Her head shot back and her eyes closed. Her core clenched around me and I was squeezed from all sides, surrounded by the softest, wettest, warmest place I never wanted to leave.

We stayed out there on that blanket in that field for hours. We switched between fucking and making love. Sometimes we just stared at one another while I was still hard inside of her body and we caught our breaths.

Sometimes we talked about everything and sometimes about nothing at all.

We came, we laughed, and we'd start all over again.

It wasn't until after midnight when I checked my phone and realized I had several missed calls from Critter. I clicked my text icon and froze. The world around me stopped. It was just me. Sawyer. And the text that glared at me hatefully from the screen in my hand.

"What is it?" Sawyer asked, turning me by the shoulder to face her.

"That was Critter." There was nothing I wanted to do less in the world then deliver the words I had to say next. I glanced up from my phone. "It's your mother. She's missing."

Sawyer gasped. "Where is..." I didn't need her to finish the sentence.

I shook my head slowly.

I wanted to save her from what I was about to tell her but couldn't. My heart broke for her before I'd even uttered the words. "We don't know."

CHAPTER 12

SAWYER

The second we landed we jumped into Finn's truck and raced over to Critter's house. Critter came out to meet us in the yard.

"What happened?" I asked feeling panic invade my entire body like an enemy I'd fought against and lost to before.

"She was on the porch. Maddy went inside to get her some tea. When she came back out your mother was gone. At first, they thought she just wandered off. But we checked the sunflower field, and there was no sign of her."

Finn chimed in. "We can split up, cover more ground that way."

Critter shook his head. "You haven't checked your phone since you landed, have you?"

"No, why? What happened?" Finn asked, looking as amped up as I was at the news.

"Because Caroline is right here. She's home. She's

safe. She got confused and wandered off. She was only gone for a handful of hours. Came back full of mud and mosquito bites. But other than that, she's okay. She's resting now."

My insides, which had felt shriveled up with the news that something happened to my mother, suddenly expanded again and I was finally able to take a deep breath of air. My first since Critter first sent word of my mother's disappearance. It was almost too much. I felt dizzy. I took one wobbly step and then another before strong arms caught me as I fell. I looked up into Finn's concerned beautiful face. He was shouting something at me, but I couldn't hear the words. I only saw his lips moving as his handsome face faded away completely until I was alone in the darkness.

Sawyer

Finn was sticking by my side closer than ever. Not just because I fainted and he freaked out but because we didn't know where Richard was. Apparently, Critter's man lost sight of him when he went into a bar and never came back out.

Finn wanted to leave again and I promised him we would go in a few days. After the scare with my mom I just needed to feel close to her and to Critter and couldn't fathom leaving again right away.

Until then, I tried to go on with life as usual and make sure that somebody in our inner circle was with me at all times. Finn was tenser than ever. Looking out the windows every few minutes. Pacing in front of the door. Flexing his long fingers and occasionally cracking his knuckles.

"You need to calm down," I said, turning over a page in my notebook.

"I will. Once we know where that fucker is."

"Pacing isn't going to find him any faster," I pointed out.

"No," he agreed, "but it makes me feel better. If I sit still, I might launch through the roof."

"So, sit. That's something I'd like to see," I teased with a wink.

Finn took his eyes from the window to roll his eyes at me. "Smart ass," he grumbled. It was the first time since our date ended that I'd seen him smile.

I felt his heavy footsteps on the ground as he leaned in over my shoulder. "What is this?" Finn asked, reaching over me to the table where I'd left my notebook open. "Is this part of your research?"

"No. It's…nothing." I tried to snatch it back, but I was too late and Finn was already silently mouthing the words.

My words.

"Sawyer." There was an awe in his voice I'd never heard before. He lowered the page and gazed up at me. His eyes filled with wonderment. *Pride.* My stomach flipped. "You wrote this?"

I bit my lip and fidgeted with the pen in my hand. "Yeah?" It came out as a question.

Finn set the notebook reverently back on the table. He reached for me, placing his hands on my face. He pressed a firm kiss to my lips that I felt all the way to the deepest part of my soul. "I didn't know you could write like that."

I shrugged. "Neither did I."

"It's really good. Like, really good. Do you have more?"

"Yes, but mostly it's just a bunch of scribbles. Art and religion are so closely connected. I never really knew that before. Paintings. Tapestries. Poetry. I loved the poetry so much I started reading all the poetry books we have here. They were...inspiring. I've been messing around with some ideas and the way the words feel to me when I write them. I feel peaceful reading them back to myself. In control when all I've ever felt was out of control."

"It's really incredible."

"This book is my favorite one." I reached for the book I kept out of order on the corner of the shelf. I'd been pulling it out at least a few times a day. I didn't want to keep getting the rolling stool out every time I wanted to reach it on the top shelf. I gently placed the book titled, POETRY OF THE HEART, on the table and opened to the Maya Angelou poem I fell in love with in the first chapter. "I read this and it made me feel something. I realize that's what the author was trying to do. Provoke an emotion. Relay a feeling. Vent and make people see inside her mind. It was...brilliant. Breathtaking. Then I thought that I might be able to do something like that too. Obviously, not like her, but like...I don't know. Me."

"I've never read anything like it." Finn held up the notebook again and much to my chagrin he again read my attempt at being creative although this time, much to my dismay, he read the words out loud.

A BIRD FELL from a tree today and sang his last song at the bottom.

Maybe, it wasn't a song.

Maybe, I was wrong.

It could have been a scream or a cry.

A call for help. A plea not to die.

I was helpless to know and helpless to help so I called it a song and I moved along.

A bird fell from a tree today and screamed his last scream at the bottom.

"TOO MORBID, RIGHT?" I cringed.

"No. At least I don't think so. It's about perception and not being able to change things. The dying bird could be anything. Any person you can't help or any situation you can't change. It's really…just wow." He wrapped his arms around me. "Just when I thought you couldn't amaze me anymore then you already have," he murmured.

His phone buzzed and he gave me a quick kiss before stepping to the back of the library by the storage area to take the call. It's the only space in the place where your words didn't echo or amplify like you were shouting into a megaphone.

The chime above the library door signaled a visitor. We didn't get many as of yet. Especially since we weren't officially open. But I wanted people to feel free to come check out our progress. I loved meeting more and more people from the town I now called home.

"We aren't open yet but feel free to look around," I called out as a familiar young woman entered, looking around as if she were lost. She had lifeless mouse brown hair pulled back in a severe bun at the nape of her neck. Her shapeless long-sleeved grey blouse and ankle-length black skirt brought reminded me of times I'd rather soon forget.

Am I seeing things?

"Sawyer?" the young woman asked like it was her who couldn't believe what she was seeing. She tentatively walked to the center of the room with her arms hanging low and her hands clasped together in front of her body. She looked me up and down before her mouth opened in what looked like surprise. Her eyebrows arched. "You look...you look so different."

It wasn't until she was standing directly in front of me only a few feet away when I finally recognized her. "Bridget?"

She nodded and flashed me a small smile. If she'd been smiling when she walked in, I probably would have never recognized her. "I didn't think you'd remember me."

Bridget had been the closest thing to a friend I ever had, but that didn't say much. Not being allowed to speak in public or within hearing distance of adults, or allowed to spend much time alone with others our own age, made it hard to forge relationships. Bridget and I were able to communicate through side glances and eye shifts, along with the occasional hushed whisper or stolen conversation.

"Of course, I remember you. What are you doing here?" I asked, wrapping my arms around her and pulling her in for a hug. I was happy to see her but my happiness quickly turned to concern. She was much thinner than I remembered. I could feel her ribcage pressed against me.

Out of the corner of my eye I spotted Finn who hastily ended his call but kept his distance, watching our interaction intently. I nodded at him to let him know that all was well, but he still didn't take his eyes from us.

Bridget stiffened in surprise and I realized my error. The hug. "I'm sorry," I said, taking a step back. "I wasn't thinking." Hugs weren't something I'd experienced from anyone other than my mother growing up. I imagined that Bridget's life was very much the same, if not worse. Her mother barely ever made eye contact with anyone. Not even her. It was amazing how quickly I'd embraced the hug as a greeting.

"It's alright. Affection always did come to you naturally. I always watched you put your hand out or step to close to someone before you'd correct yourself." She laughed nervously. I did too.

"You were very observant."

She looked around the room. "It wasn't like there is much else to do but look when no one thinks you're looking. Speaking of looks. You look so different than the last time I saw you. At your mother's funeral," Bridget said, looking me up and down yet again.

It was more of a curiosity than a compliment, but I thanked her anyway.

I tugged on the cut-off hem of my black denim shorts which barely covered any leg at all, suddenly feeling very exposed. "Yes, things have most certainly changed for me," I said.

"Yes. I left after that."

"I thought you were dead."

"Why?"

"Because, your father told us you were dead. Killed yourself just like your mother had." She trained her eyes on me. "I didn't believe him for one moment. I knew you were stronger than that."

Suddenly it occurred to me that she might not be alone. "Bridget, I'm happy to see you, but why are you here?" I asked, looking to Finn who was already peeking through all the windows. "*How* are you here?"

"Oh, don't worry. I'm alone. They think I'm passing out flyers for the tent service," she said, her spine straightening slightly. Her eyes finally meeting mine, if only for a second. "You're not the only rebel to come out of God's Light, you know."

I smiled. "Then where are your flyers?" I asked, eyeing her empty hands.

Bridget smiled sheepishly and whispered, "I tossed them in the nearest dumpster." A small laugh escaped her mouth and she immediately covered it and composed herself although I could see how proud she was of her defiance.

I was proud of her too.

"You're right. Maybe I'm not the only rebel to come out of the church," I commented. "But as happy as I am to see you again, Bridget, why are you here?"

"I...came to find you. I overheard some of the elders, including your father, talking about you. He told us all you were dead but I heard him correct himself to Pastor Dimitri. He told him that you were dead to him. Not like DEAD dead. Then he said you were nearby and that..."

Dread. Pure dread filled my body. I felt chills and sweats at the same time as my entire being registered the fear mounting in my heart and mind.

"And that what?" I said, egging her on, trying to remain impassive.

"And that we would all see you again real soon," she whispered to the ground.

Finn stiffened but made no move to come forward. "What...what else did he say?" I asked, trying to come off as calm as possible.

Bridget shifted from one foot to the other. "I..."

An unfamiliar male voice called to her from just outside the window. "Bridget, where did you go? Bridget, where are you? We've got work to do!"

"I have to go," she said, scurrying toward the door. She placed her hand on the handle. "That's my husband."

"Husband? Bridget, what husband?" I asked. "You don't have to go. I can help you. You can stay. I'll protect you if you want to stay."

"You were always foolish, Sawyer. You of all people should know better." Bridget shook her head and scurried over to the door, not giving Finn so much as a second glance as she passed him on the way. Her shoulders were now hunched, her eyes downcast. The God's Light traditional uniform for women. "No one can protect me."

"Wait! Don't leave. What else did you have to tell me?" I asked, feeling the panic in my chest growing.

Bridget glanced up at me with sympathy in her weary eyes. "Sandy Bennett. Remember Sandy Bennett."

"Bridget where are you!" the voice outside grew louder and angrier. She opened the door and the outside light temporarily blinded me.

"Wait, Bridget!!" I called again. But I was too late.

She was already gone.

CHAPTER 13

FINN

I left Sawyer with Josh at the bar because Critter insisted that we needed to talk. Maddy, the nurse, was with Sawyer's mother and when I asked if she was enough security Critter informed me that she was more security than actual nurse and that he and I quote 'wouldn't fuck with her.'

"Where are we going?" I asked Critter who pulled up the airboat behind my shack and barely slowed down so I could jump on board. "I thought you wanted to talk?"

"I'm moving my lips and sounds coming out, right? Ain't that talking?" Critter spat, turning the boat and heading into the swamp at speeds that anyone who hadn't grown up here wouldn't dare try.

"That girl who came in. Bridget. She gave us a name. Josh is running it and looking into it. Let's see where that takes us before we do something that is gonna keep you separated from your family for another twenty-two years."

Critter's glare burned a hole in my skull. "I've been waiting twenty-two fucking years for this bastard to roll-on back into my swamp and you best believe I'm gonna make sure he ain't ever leaving."

"What exactly is your plan then?"

"Good old-fashioned southern hospitality," Critter answered gruffly.

Shit.

"And that means what?"

"That means I'm gonna shoot his head off his shoulders and then I'm gonna light a cigar. Maybe later, I'll celebrate with some pie."

"All right. Go in. Blow his head off. Got it. Sounds like a hell of a plan."

"No. You weren't listening. There was also that bit about a cigar and pie."

I rested my head in my hands. "Critter. I want this asshole gone as much as the next guy. But you just got Caroline back. If we get caught, we're right back where you started and it'll be *you* paying the price for Richard's crimes. *AGAIN.* Don't let him win. Not this time. Don't you want to see her when she gets better? Talk to her? Then we have to be smart about this. I'm not saying that southern hospitality is off the table. I'm just saying that maybe we don't want to rush into a church and blow the pastor away while he's preaching at the pulpit like some dumb ass redneck militia of two."

Critter rolled his eyes. "Don't be so dramatic, *Karen.*" He scoffed. "Ain't you ever killed a man before? I've served in two tours and I tell ya, it takes a little more finesse than just popping a cap in his ass or whatever you kids say nowadays."

"I don't know a single person who says that," I groaned. "Except maybe Miller."

Critter looked out into the dark waters before us. "I've known men like him before. He's not going to stop until they are back under his control or dead. And since we know he's not going to get his control...he's gotta go," Critter said with a mixture of both anger and sadness. "He's lucky he isn't already dead, but he was a hard man to find. Covered his tracks well, hiding behind that church of his. I had several PI's look into him over the years. They couldn't come up with shit until the last one came back and told me Richard and Caroline were both dead. Car accident." Critter closed his eyes briefly like he was remembering a pain that was too much to bear. "I thought she was dead. I thought my world was dead." His hands tightened on the wheel. "Now I realize that my PI must have found Richard and that fucker paid him off to feed me false information. That son of a bitch PI better hope he never crosses paths with me again."

We moved over a patch of ground like it was water. But when I saw the next patch in the distance I stood and squinted like I couldn't believe what I was seeing.

"Shit," I swore. There was something lying right in front of the boat. "Stop, Critter!" I screamed, directing his attention at the clump of hair and fabric.

Critter swerved sharply and knocked me into the water. I waded over to the grass and pulled myself up only to see that the thing we were about to hit wasn't a thing at all.

It was a person. Someone I'd seen just hours before. The same person who'd delivered the warning that Richard was here.

Bridget.

SAWYER

Angry. I was so beyond angry.

All I saw was red. Bright blood red.

On the inside, I was a car skidding to a screeching halt on a wet road. On the outside, I was a fake soft smile and elevator music.

"Who did this to you?" Josh asked, gently. There was a lot of sympathy in her voice as she patiently waited for a banged up and bruised Bridget to answer the questions she'd asked several times already without a single muttered response. "We're trying to help you," Josh continued. She was in full cop mode, but her compassion for the woman in the hospital bed between us surprised me.

"Bridget, I told you. We can help you. We can protect you. Look at me. I'm here, aren't I? They are keeping me safe. They can keep you safe too," I reassured her, placing my hand on her arm that wasn't in a sling. Bridget stared at my hand as if I was burning her. I jerked it back and rubbed it like I was dousing the flame.

"Not for long," she groaned, her one eye purple and swollen shut. She was banged up bad and we had no idea how she'd gotten to be lying in the middle of the swamp but she'd live.

For now.

"Bridget, if you go back there," I trailed off, knowing exactly what would happen. This was a warning for coming to me. She could have died. They wouldn't have cared.

Monsters parading themselves around as Christians.

"What if I could—" Josh started when two men entered the room. The first man I didn't recognize at all, but he was wearing the Church of God's Light pin on his shirt. The second one stayed behind the door in the shadow with his hat low on his head.

"Don't answer anything," the first man commanded, coming to stand at Bridget's side. "This is my wife."

"Funny," Josh said, standing up to reveal her full police uniform. Her badge glinted under the fluorescent light. She scrunched her lips. "I didn't hear a 'thank God you're all right.' I didn't even hear a 'I was worried sick.' The only thing I did here was you proclaiming that she was your wife like you're collecting your dog from the pound." Josh pointed to Bridget's eye. "This how you treat your dog, sir?"

"I'm in shock. That's all," the man said, picking up Bridget's hand awkwardly like he'd never done it before. "How dare you accuse me of treating her like a dog."

"No, I believe I indicated you treated her like less than a dog."

"Can we talk later, *officer*," the word dripped off his tongue in disdain. "I'd like a moment alone with my wife."

"Only if it's okay with our *victim*," Josh said using the same stress on the word victim.

Bridget didn't meet our eyes but nodded. "It's okay. This is my husband."

"Bridget, you don't have to talk to them!" I cried as Josh moved toward the door. "We can stay. You don't have to be alone with them. Ever again." Josh turned me around by my shoulders and guided me from the room, shutting the door behind us.

"We can't leave her in there with them!" I shouted. "They're monsters. Look what they did to her!"

"They ain't gonna do shit with me standing out here." She placed a hand on her belt. "I got a gun and shit. What are they gonna do. Fight me with some bullshit prayers? Sawyer, if they touch one hair on that girl's head, I'll go in their shooting like it's the wild wild west up in here." Her eyes were strong and serious.

"Thank you," I said, grateful that I wasn't the only one trying to protect her.

"But there is something you must know," Josh said, keeping her eyes trained on the door.

"What?" I asked.

She sighed and pointed to the window where Bridget's husband was huddled over her bed. "That girl in there is gonna walk out of this hospital with them tonight."

"No!" I shouted, feeling sick at the thought.

"What they did to her was a warning and she got the message loud and clear. Not even a blink or wink or shake of her hand to tell me otherwise."

"No…!" I said, reaching for the handle. "My mother stayed with the man who tortured her. I'm not going to stand back and watch it happen again. I can't, I won't!"

118

Josh pulled me back and set me down on the chair in the hallway. She crouched down so only I could hear her. "You need to realize they aren't all as strong as you."

The door opened and the familiar feeling of dread dripped down my spine as the men walked past me. I couldn't bother looking up at them. I was too disgusted to give them that much. "We'll be back," Bridget's husband said almost cheerily, like he was bragging. "To bring her *home*."

When the bell chimed and the doors slid open, both men climbed inside. Before they slid shut again the other man spoke. The one who'd lingered in the shadows.

"Yes. We will be back. To bring *them* home."

CHAPTER 14

FINN

I wish I could unsee the mangled girl lying between the reeds in the swamp. I wanted to wash Bridget's image from my brain because it was all I could see except every time the image came to me it wasn't Bridget I saw lying there bloodied and broken.

It was Sawyer.

The thought made me sick. I had to pull over twice on the way to Critter's to purge the thought via the entire contents of my stomach. After heaving onto the road, I banged out my frustrations with my fists on my steering wheel. Screaming my rage out to absolutely no one.

Critter was out back of the bar puffing on his cigar and directing a liquor truck that was backing up to the door.

"A little early this morning?" I asked him as the driver of the truck hopped out and handed him a clipboard before sliding open the back door and pulling out the metal ramp.

"Is it? I hadn't noticed," Critter said.

"Maybe if you got some sleep you would."

"Too busy thinkin' to sleep," he said, taking a puff of his cigar.

I'd known the man my entire life. I used to steal sunflowers from the field around his house when I was still in diapers. Never once do I remember him appearing tired until that morning. I was too young when Sawyer's mother left to remember how he handled it all although I'm sure he looked just as tired then.

"Anything you'd like to share with me?" I asked, hoping that maybe by talking I could ease his mind a bit.

Critter followed the drive ramp and inspected the shipment. He scribbled his signature on the paperwork, handing it back to the driver who tucked it away and started unloading. Critter, never one to sit idly by, grabbed a box and followed him into the bar, dropping it in the storage area next to the office. I followed and did the same. "Nothing you'd want to hear," he grumbled.

"Try me," I said.

Critter grabbed another box from the truck. I was bending over to grab one myself when he turned to me, dropped the box and reached into his pocket to pull out his phone. He pressed a few numbers and held up the screen so I could see his contacts pulled up to someone listed only as 911-B. "What is that? Or *who* is that?"

"This," he said, tucking the phone back into his jeans, "is a number I could call and with one flick of my thumb I could have Richard Dixon wiped off the face of the fucking planet now that I know where he is."

"Then, why haven't you?" I asked curiously.

"Because she asked me not to," Critter said, rubbing his hand on his face.

"What?"

Critter grabbed another box. "Caroline. Last night she had a moment of clarity. A longer one than usual. She told me it wouldn't make me no better than him if I had his filthy blood on my hands. She made me promise I wouldn't and now I gotta figure out how to put an end to that son of a bitch's reign of terror some other way."

"We," I corrected him. "WE have to figure out how to end it."

Critter grunted. "How's Sawyer holding up after seeing him at the hospital?"

"She keeps saying she's okay but I know she isn't. I wouldn't be if I was in the same room as the very man who kidnapped her mother, threatened both of their lives and tormented for years?" Even saying the words made me downright murderous myself, but I saw how Critter was teetering on the edge and didn't want to be the one to tip him over and have him break his promise to his wife.

"Yeah, I'm aware of the man's resume," Critter snapped. "But thanks for the update though. It's always nice to have a refresher course in all things awful about the man I've imagined killing for a couple decades plus."

"He ain't exactly on the list of people Sawyer and I

will be inviting to our wedding," I said without thinking.

Critter turned to me and shot me a glare like I was the enemy. I turned around to make sure Richard wasn't standing behind me. "What?" I asked.

He narrowed his eyes at me. "You serious about that? You thinking of marrying *my* daughter?"

I thought about my next words carefully, but the answer was a simple one and it wasn't a day to be lying to Critter. "Yeah. Yes." I grimaced. "Sir?"

"Son…"

"It's *son* now?"

"Yeah, it is." Critter pointed at me, wagging his finger as he spoke. "*Son*, if you go and hurt my girl in *any* way, I'm telling you right this fuckin' second that I'll skin you alive, feed your carcass to my hunting dogs, and mount what's left of you above my front door as a warning to others." He ruffled my hair like he used to do when I was a kid and I didn't like it now as much as I hated it back then. I smoothed it back down and Critter smiled, going about wiping down the bar and glasses like he didn't just threaten my life in a very real and gruesome way.

"Wow, Critter. It's been awhile since I've gotten a good dad-style talking to. I have to say though, I never expected it from you," I said, going back to the business of helping him and the delivery man carry in the boxes.

"Well, don't be expecting it again 'cause that was a courtesy warning. You'll only be getting the one."

"Noted."

"What's this?" Critter asked when the driver handed him a bottle of whiskey that hadn't been in any of the boxes. He turned the clear bottle around in his hands.

The driver shrugged. "I was told to give it to you by the boss. It's a gift. A sample for you to try. Something new he'll be trying to sell you, I suppose. Not sure. I just deliver the booze, impregnate my wife, and keep paying for these damned kids' tuition. Not necessarily in that order."

"Thanks, Pete. Tell Mike this better not be no Yankee shit. The last bottle he sent me I used as target practice in my field."

Pete turned the bottle over in Critter's hand. Taped to the back was a note that said. NOT YANKEE SHIT.

Critter chuckled.

"Southern all the way, Critter," Pete said. He jogged off and climbed into his truck. I followed Critter into the empty bar.

He placed the cigar in his mouth and opened the bottle of whiskey, setting down two glasses. He filled them both over halfway. He slid one toward me. "It's a whiskey kind of morning."

"I've never known you to be a whiskey for breakfast kind of man."

"You also never knew I was married and had a daughter."

"Good point."

Critter clinked his glass to mine without waiting for me to pick mine up. He emptied it in two large swallows, slamming it down on the bar so hard I was surprised it didn't break.

I spun around the glass I'd yet to take a sip from

while Critter was already pouring another. "What about the name that Bridget girl gave Sawyer?"

"Sandy Bennett," I said. "Josh is on it. Running the name through as many agencies as she has access to.

Critter drained his second glass. He sighed. "You know, from the second I found out Caroline and Sawyer were alive I had to put my need to hurt that mother-fucker second to my need to want to crack his skull open. You know why? Because family comes first. My girls come first. But unfortunately, Caroline was right. You were…well, sort of right. I ain't going to prison when I just got my family back. I ain't living without them again." His expression softened. "I can't."

I looked up to him. "I get it," I said, running my hand through my hair and blowing out a breath of frustration. I'd had the same thought myself a thousand times. My chest panged. I remember the hurt I carried around after Jackie died. Enough to send me into years of solitude. Critter had known what that felt like and he'd reached out to me but even he couldn't break through to me.

"The way I see it is that you and I are in the same boat. We've both had some horrible losses," Critter said, echoing my thoughts. "I think it's about damned time we're due for a win. Or a break. *Or something.*"

I shook my head and traced my finger around the top of my glass. "It's insane how one man could cause all this grief. All this heartache. You'd think there was an army of him out there. Or that he was the devil himself."

Critter rested both hands on the bar and closed his eyes for a moment like he was wrestling with something. When he opened his eyes again, he spoke with more conviction than I'd ever heard him talk about anything before. "I have news for you," Critter said. He coughed and tapped his chest with his closed fist. "Richard Dixon *is* the devil himself."

Critter's face paled and his eyes went wide. He started coughing. When it didn't subside, I stood up and rounded the bar. He was pounding on his chest with his closed fist. He grabbed the counter for support but lost his grip and I caught him as he fell, lowering him to the ground as he gasped for air. His eyes glazed over. I reached for my phone in a panic. My mind not able to catch up to the events at hand.

"Stay with me, Critter. You've made it through so much you will not give up on me now, old man."

Critter stared up at the ceiling, unfocused. His eyes began to close.

The tings overhead fluttered all around the ceiling indicating the door had been opened. With my phone to my ear, I glanced up to find Sawyer standing next to me looking down at Critter.

She choked back a sob. "Nooooo!" she cried.

My heart sank. For him. For her.

Then...he stopped breathing.

CHAPTER 15

SAWYER

The hospital was the last place I wanted to be again.

Seeing Critter.

Critter was strong. Healthy. The most stubborn man I ever knew. But also, the most caring. The most loving. I loved everything about him from his deep baritone voice to his ridiculous mustache, which only he could pull off.

When I was there to see Bridget, I wanted to help her save herself.

With Critter lying there. Hooked to the tubes and machines. I wanted to not just save him, I wanted to breathe life into him. I wanted to pound on his chest with my closed fists and scream at him until he woke up and told me he was going to be okay.

He *had* to be okay.

HAD. TO. BE. OKAY.

Finn stood in the corner talking to Critter's doctor

while I sat by Critter's bedside, holding his hand with my head on his chest.

"So that's about it," the doctor said. I'd been so involved in my own devastation that I hadn't heard a word she's said to Finn.

"I'm sorry, I don't understand, what exactly are you saying?" I asked. "Was it a heart attack?" I picked my head up from Critter's chest but kept my fingers laced through his.

The doctor looked at me over the rim of her glasses. She tucked her clipboard underneath her arm. I knew whatever she was about to tell me wasn't going to be good since Finn was now leaning on the wall for support. His face several shades paler than it had been when we got there.

I stilled. I could hear my heart beating when she spoke.

"The short version?" the doctor asked like she was in a hurry.

I nodded and held my breath.

"Your father was poisoned."

CHAPTER 16

SAWYER

POISONED.

F inn and I hadn't left the hospital in over two days. We slept upright, propped up against each other in chairs. We held each other, not just physically but emotionally. We were beyond tired and I could tell the stress was weighing on him just as much as it was weighing on me. He loved Critter like a father and I loved Critter before even knowing he was my father.

I found myself mentally chanting 'please wake up please wake up please wake up.' Every time the machine beeped, my hopes would soar that it was a sign he was waking up.

And every time my hopes were dashed when he didn't.

"No matter what, we're going to get through this together," Finn said. I loved how he was trying to comfort me when he was feeling the same despair I was. "Do you want to go get something to eat? It's been awhile since you've had anything."

I shook my head. "No. I'm just going to stay right here. With him." I brought my knees up to my chest and wrapped my arms around my legs.

"You know, staring at him like a line in the water, waiting for something to happen isn't going to make him get better any faster," Finn said, trying to coax a smile from me.

I kept my eyes on Critter. "I just want him to wake up."

"You heard the doctor. He's got a fighting shot. He strong. He'll make it through. I know he will," Finn said and either he was a really good actor or he truly believed what he was saying.

"How can you be so sure?" I asked, feeling my eyes grow heavier and heavier. Feeling the lump in my throat and heart swell with each passing second.

Finn slid out of his chair and knelt before me. "Remember when we had a conversation about faith? I believe you told me that the dictionary defined it as 'the belief in something based on spiritual apprehension rather than proof.'"

I nodded. Although it killed me to tear my eyes away from Critter's resting body for even a moment, I knew I wanted to look down at Finn. I didn't need to just hear what he was trying to tell me. I needed to FEEL it.

He gathered my hands in his. "That's why I am sure he's going to pull through. I don't believe in much. But I have faith in him. That man has waited a long time to be with his family. Trust me. He ain't leaving you now."

"He always was a stubborn ox."

Finn and I both looked to the door where my mother was being wheeled in by Maddy. "Mo...Hi," I corrected. There was a clarity about her but I wanted to veer on the side of caution so I stop myself from calling her Mom.

Maddy wheeled her up to Critters bed then stepped out of the room, standing guard by the door.

With tears in her eyes, my mother held out her hand to me. "Come here, baby. Come sit with your mother for a while."

I hadn't ever heard my mother sound that strong, that *clear*.

Was this temporary? Was she back? My thoughts, stomach, and mind tumbled together wreaking havoc on my heartbeat.

For a moment, I just stood there. Staring. Gawking. It was like she wasn't even the same woman. My mother wiggled her outstretched fingers. "I've got you now. I promise."

It was those words that broke whatever barrier was still holding me back from my mother. I felt an immediate rush of overwhelming elation. Of peace. The invisible chain of our mother-daughter bond was being repaired link by link with every step I took toward her. I could feel it in my bones.

In my heart.

Finn stepped aside so I could kneel next to my mother, but that wasn't close enough for her. She reached over and tugged on my arm. "Come here," she said, pulling me down onto her lap. She lifted my feet over the edge of her wheelchair and cradled me like a baby. I lost it. Sobbing into my mother's white blouse as she brushed the hair back from my forehead. I sobbed out my job. My frustration. My confusion. My love. She whispered to me how much she loved me as I gave her all the tears I'd been holding back my entire life.

After I'd settled down, I stayed there on my mother's lap and together we watched Critter's chest rise and fall with the help of the machines.

"I'll let you two have some time alone," Finn said, excusing himself.

My mother stopped him before he could get to the door. "Are you the young man my daughter is so desperately in love with?" The question made my insides smile. It was the same way I felt visiting Finn's parents. Like this was the way things should've been all along. With just a few words my mother was telling me she was not just my mother again, but the mother she'd always wanted to be.

I felt stronger because of her. I wanted to BE stronger because of her.

Finn smiled. He appeared completely unaffected by her comment while even my insides were blushing.

"Yes, ma'am. That would be me," Finn said. "It's nice to officially meet you, ma'am. Although, I guess we've met before. It's been a lot of years."

My mother nodded. "It has been a lot of years. You've grown a bit since the last time I saw you," my mother teased, but her voice remained sad and heavy.

"Just a little, I suppose."

I crawled off my mother and took a chair next to her. She linked her hand with mine like she'd done it a million times. I looked down at where our hands were connected and I still couldn't believe it was all real. "You used to steal her sunflowers," I said to Finn, recalling what my mother had told me during our first conversation.

"He sure did," she confirmed.

"I guess all of my secrets are out now," Finn said, rocking back on his heels.

"Critter is very happy that you and Sawyer found each other," my mother said, looking between Finn and Critter.

He was?

Finn's smile was a sad one. "That's nice to hear. The last conversation we had about me and Sawyer ended with him telling me that he was gonna...well, we don't need to get into it here let's just say it ends with me in parts."

"He threatened you?" I asked, both shocked and secretly elated that Critter was so protective over me when he'd known Finn his entire life and had only met me a few months before.

"Of course," Finn said, leaning against the wall. "That's what good fathers do to protect their daughters. I'd expect nothing less than the threat of an ass-kicking every other week at the very least."

My mother looked over to Critter. "He'll live to threaten another day. Because just like you, Finn, I have faith that he is going to pull through. I can feel it." She placed her hand over her chest.

Finn excused himself again to the cafeteria where he told me he was going to get me some food whether I liked it or not.

"Two decades and this still isn't over yet," my

mother sighed. "But it needs to be over. It needs to end now." There was a determination in her eyes when she said out loud the thoughts I'd been thinking all along.

My mother continued and I found myself nodding along to everything she was saying. I grew angrier and angrier with each sentence she spoke. "After all these years, one man has still found a way to terrorize this family, despite all he's already put us through. It's still not enough. Keeping me against my will wasn't enough. Threatening my family wasn't good enough. Poisoning my husband…" she paused and composed herself. "It's the final straw. I'm tired of standing by and doing nothing. He's not going to stop. It will never be enough…" her voice trailed off. "It will never be enough until we're all dead."

"And yet there doesn't seem to be a single thing we can do about it," I said, my frustrations bubbling up to the surface all over again.

"Or maybe, there is," she whispered, the corner of her lip turning upward in a half smile. She took a deep breath and suddenly stood up from her wheelchair. I leapt up, half-expecting to have to catch her if she fell. But she didn't fall. She straightened her shoulders and walked over to Critter's bedside like a queen ready to take care of the kingdom while the King was temporarily unable. She lifted his hand to hers and kissed it before covering it with her other hand.

This was a woman whose will, who's very being had been burnt to ashes and yet here she was, ready to fight for her family. The determination radiating off her was almost tangible. I felt proud. I felt my own resolve to fight build from within me all over again.

For the first time in a long time, I had a feeling that everything was okay. I guess you could even say that I had faith. And just maybe it was because of that faith that a deep voice bellowed from the bed behind me.

"What in the hell is all the fuss about?"

CHAPTER 17

FINN

I came into the room to find Critter awake and alert. He looked between Caroline and Sawyer then back again. He smiled, his mustache turning upward.

"Now I told you not to make a fuss," he groaned, adjusting his position on the bed, trying to sit up higher.

Sawyer leaned down and wrapped her arms around Critter. Her shoulders shook with her joy, making my own heart skip a few beats and the tears prick the back of my eyes.

I may have grown up surrounded by these people, but to find out that Sawyer was related to Critter was probably the best news I'd ever heard, despite his threats toward me.

Because now it wasn't just my family. It was OUR family.

"Hey, Mama. Hey, kiddo," Critter, wrapping one arm around Sawyer and the other Caroline.

"It's so beautiful, man."

I looked over to Miller who was sobbing at the sight. Tears streaming down his face. Strings of saliva connecting his teeth.

I laughed because I couldn't NOT laugh.

Josh rolled her eyes and dragged Miller from the room. "Let's let them have some time. You can come talk to him later," she told him.

"You promise?" Miller squeaked as Josh led him from the room with a wave over her shoulder.

The doctor showed up just as they left. The same one who saw Critter on the first day he was brought in by ambulance. "How are you feeling?" she asked Critter, checking numbers on a machine above his head.

Critter winced as Caroline adjusted his pillow. He continued to wince until he was settled back against them again.

"How am I feeling?" Critter repeated, his bushy eyebrows reaching into his forehead. "Like I'm in a goddamned hospital. But I'm alive. So, there's that."

"You are," Caroline said. "You're here."

"And so are you, baby."

The looks they were exchanging were so full of love I thought immediately of my father's words. Critter and Caroline had that forever factor he spoke about. I looked to Sawyer and I could see our future together. Our lives spent here in Outskirts. If I hadn't known it before I knew it then. Sawyer was always meant to be my forever. And I was always meant to be hers.

"I never thought I'd talk to you again," Sawyer admitted. "When they were carting you away..." she paused.

"Sorry I scared you," Critter said. "I won't do it again. I promise."

The doctor started to ramble off something using words like toxicity, ingesting, countermeasures, and just in time. She finished with, "You're lucky to be alive."

"Thanks, Doc," Critter said. "But what the hell happened? Should I worry about it happening again?"

We all stiffened. All of us of course except for the doctor who simply shrugged and kept her eyes trained on her clipboard. "Not unless you plan on being poisoned again any time soon."

The room was dead silent as Critter's eyes slowly widened. His fists curled up into balls on the bed. The only noise in that room was the echo of the doctor's heels as she marched down the hall.

And the sound of Critter's blood boiling.

CHAPTER 18

SAWYER

It had been a few weeks since Critter was released from the hospital. Since then Josh was working with my mother and Critter to make their case against Richard. They didn't involve me. They said it was best if I knew as little as possible about what they were up to.

Finn still wanted to skip town. I still wanted to stay and be close to my family, and I still had to make sure someone was with me at all times as a safety measure.

At least Critter was home now. And with him and my mother getting better every day (she hadn't slipped back to thinking it was two decades ago at all since the hospital) I felt relieved. But there was something else nagging me. Something I couldn't quite put my finger on.

After all the events of the last few months, I felt utterly run down.

I pulled out a chair from one of the tables and sat down, propping my feet up on another. Since Critter was out spending time with my mother, Josh had volunteered to put in some hours after her police shift. As did Finn who was in the back-cleaning dishes and Miller, who was out back taking a delivery.

Speaking of which, the delivery man who'd delivered the whiskey they believed poisoned Critter disappeared with his family and hadn't been seen since that morning.

Coward.

"Why does it take four of us to do the job of one man?" I asked Josh who was refilling napkin dispensers.

"I knew that man was a machine but damn. He really does do it all."

I tried to laugh but I was too tired to conjure up the energy.

"You don't seem like yourself lately. Is it your mother? Critter?" Josh asked. Her gold bangle bracelets clanked as she reached over and set her hand on top of mine. Her smile was genuine but sad. Lines of concern were etched all over her usually smooth and perfect face.

I shook my head just as another wave of nausea washed over me. Churning my stomach, threatening to force out everything I'd eaten that morning. I closed my eyes and took a few deep breaths until, thankfully, the threat subsided.

I waited a few beats to make sure the feeling was completely gone before I spoke. "No, it's not my mother or Critter. I just haven't been feeling great. I think I ate something bad."

"Again? There's no way someone eats something

bad that often." Josh rounded the table and pulled up a chair next to mine. "Like HOW have you not been feeling great?" she asked, scooting her chair closer until her knees were against my thigh.

"It's nothing," I said, waving her off. "I'm just a little lightheaded." Just thinking about throwing up made me woozy. "But I haven't thrown up," I added, like that would make all the difference in my diagnosis.

"That's not specific enough, Say." Josh leaned back and placed her feet on the same chair as mine. "What else have you been feeling?" she asked with a casual shrug, looking down at her nails. "Don't leave anything out."

I took a moment to think. "Uh...there are some other things," I said quietly.

"What kind of other things?" Josh asked ten times as loud as if her yelling would make me speak up.

I looked around to make sure Miller and Finn weren't around. "Things...things I don't feel comfortable talking about."

Josh nodded like she understood and pulled her feet from the chair, leaning in closer. "What if I list some common symptoms of some things and you just nod or shake your head?" she asked. "Would that be easier?"

"I can do that," I said, feeling a lot more comfortable with her idea.

"Are you...sore anywhere?" she asked, refilling the napkin dispenser at the table we were sitting at.

I nodded.

"Okay. Do any of those areas include your tender lady areas? You know, breasts? Vagina? Both?"

I nodded again.

"Do you feel more tired than usual?" she asked. "Never mind. I can answer that one. It's a yes. Those bags under your eyes weren't built in a day."

She was right. "I'm too tired to feel insulted."

"Do you find yourself more sensitive to smells lately?"

"Not that I'm aware of," I said, adding, "although you sprayed enough of that disinfectant on this table to use it in a hospital."

"Okay, how about this one, have you had your period in the last month?" Josh asked.

I thought about her question but couldn't give a definitive answer. "I'm not sure. I've never really kept track. Although, it hasn't been recently, so it's possible I haven't had it in a while."

"Like what's a while?"

"Well, I've been here for over three months. I don't remember getting it since I've been here," I said.

Josh looked at me, turning her head and nodding like she was waiting for me to come to a conclusion I wasn't coming to. "And? What do you think?" I asked. "Flu?"

Josh leaned forward and placed a hand on each of my knees. "Sawyer, do you think there is any possibility that you could be pregnant?"

I almost laughed as I shook my head. "No. It's not possible."

"What do you mean it's not possible? Don't even try and lie and say that you and Finn aren't bumping uglies." Josh crossed her arms over her chest.

"If bumping uglies means what I think it means then yes. We are. But I can't get pregnant."

146

"And why is that?" Josh asked.

"Because Finn and I aren't married." As soon as the words left my mouth, I realized how stupid that sounded. I was reciting something I'd been taught at an early age. Something I never even considered to challenge. Except, if I'd spent any time thinking about it at all I would have come to the conclusion I'd just came to in about twenty seconds. Not only wasn't that true. It was downright ridiculous. "I know, I know," I groaned. "I just realized how stupid that sounded too."

Josh looked like she was contemplating her words as she bit the inside of her cheek. She spoke slowly. Cautiously. "Sawyer, I don't know what you were taught, but it is possible for a man to get a woman pregnant without them being married. If you don't believe me, just ask my cousin Corinne. She's got a baby daddy in every county from here to Miami."

A pit in my stomach began to grow. I placed my hands over where I'd unbuttoned the top button of my shorts that very morning getting ready for work. I remember blaming their snugness on shrinkage from the wrong dryer setting.

"Have you ever seen an episode of Teen Mom?"

"Uh. No."

"Let me ask you this. Do you and Finn use anything while you get down to business?" Josh asked.

Use anything? Like what?

I blew out a long-frustrated breath. I felt my skin tingling. A warning of impending feeling overload. "I don't know. Are there other things to use besides your...you know. Your parts?"

Josh knelt in front of me and pressed her lips

together to keep from laughing. She tapped my leg with each option she listed. "I meant like birth control. Condoms? Pills? Pulling out?"

"Not that I'm aware of," I answered.

Josh sighed. "Baby girl, this is my fault. I knew you and Finn were getting closer. I should have had the birds and bees talk with you."

"You use bees?" I asked, my eyes widening. "How?"

"You have got to be kidding me!" Josh exclaimed.

"Okay, that one was a joke," I admitted. "But I still don't know what you mean." I was trying to play it off. Trying to make a joke of it all, but the reality was that I'd never been so embarrassed in my life.

"It's just an expression. A pretty stupid one now that I think about it."

I growled, hating that I was still so naive about the world. I thought I was doing well for someone who didn't grow up in the mainstream USA immersed in pop culture.

I was wrong.

I was embarrassed above all else.

Of course, you could get pregnant even if you weren't married. Marriage wasn't some magic fertility ritual.

"Oh," I sat up. "I might be pregnant."

I might be pregnant.

"It just now occurred to you?" Josh asked, slapping me on the arm with a folded-up napkin.

"Apparently, I'm slow at catching on," I said.

There could be a baby inside of me. OUR baby. A life that depends on me. A spark of what I could only describe as unconditional love planted deep inside of me and with each passing second it grew until I was practically humming with love for this baby I hadn't even known if I was really carrying yet.

"It takes two to tango, Sawyer. Finn was there too."

Yes, he was.

Uh oh. Finn. What was Finn going to think when I told him that because of my stupidity I could be pregnant with his baby?

An odd sort of thrill jolted through me and I found myself fighting a smile. He'd said he wanted kids someday. With me. I took a deep calming breath. Which was perfect timing because the back door opened and Finn sauntered in, draping his sweat-drenched shirt across the back of his neck and shoulders.

The second he saw me he knew something was going on. I must have had panic written all over my face.

"Shit. What the hell happened?" Finn asked. "What's wrong, Say?" He crossed the bar and crouched down where Josh had just been. She stood up to make room for him, leaning up against the bar.

I covered my face with my hands but he gently pulled them away and tipped my face up so our eyes met. I shook my head. Embarrassed that even if I could find the words that I still wouldn't be able to relay them properly. "I can't. I just can't."

"What happened?" Finn repeated his question, this time to Josh and in a much harsher tone.

Josh didn't crack a joke or even smile. She remained serious, yet calm. Her voice softening to a tone I'd never heard her use before. I could tell she was trying very hard not to make me feel worse than I already did. "Sawyer hasn't been feeling well."

"Still?" Finn asked. "Stomach flu? Cold? I'll run to the general store. What can I get you? Or better yet, we'll just take you to the doctor down the street. He does walk-ins. Come on, let's go." He stood and pulled me up with him as he looked me over for obvious signs of sickness.

I looked to Josh for help. Pleading with my eyes to not make me be the one to tell him. I was being a coward but I'd been so strong in other areas. I could bomb at bravery at this one little thing.

"Wait," she said, tugging on Finn's shirt. "Take a seat."

Finn reluctantly sat and I did the same. "Is someone going to tell me what's going on?"

"Sawyer, doesn't quite remember when the last time aunt flow came to town, but she doesn't think it was this month," she said. "Or since she's been in Outskirts."

I winced.

Finn's entire demeanor became stone.

I cringed and waited for him to pull his hands from mine, but he didn't. "Why didn't you say something?" he asked gently, giving my hands a squeeze.

I felt my face reddening. "I didn't know. I didn't think it was possible. I feel so stupid."

"Why?" Finn stroked my hair. When I went to put my head down again he wouldn't let me. "Look at me, Say." Finn was smiling, laughing at my wanting to hide my face from him. "Why do you feel stupid? Come on. Look at me."

I slowly looked up. Our eyes met. "I just thought I wasn't feeling good." I pressed my lips together and paused. "And I didn't think it was a possibility because...I thought..." I spit the last words out like rapid fire. The fastest sentence I'd ever spoken in my life. "I thought you had to be married to get pregnant." Even I had to laugh this time. "See? I'm stupid. And therefore, I find myself to be very *very* embarrassed right now."

"Hey," Finn said, his voice taking on an angry tone. "You're not stupid and I don't want to hear you ever say that about yourself again." His nostrils flared. He pulled me from my chair onto his lap.

"Josh, can you do us a favor? Can you go to the general store and..."?

"Already on it," Josh called from the front door where her purse was already slung around her shoulder. "Be right back," she called and then she was gone.

"I don't really know what to say," I confessed. "But it would explain why these shorts don't fit anymore." I looked down to my unhooked button.

Finn smiled. "We'll get you some new ones." His smile dropped as he snaked his hand up my thigh. He made his way to my stomach where he pushed the material of my t-shirt up and placed a hand on my belly. "I hope you're in there," he whispered.

My heart fluttered in my chest like it grew wings and was trying to escape. That's when I realized. I hoped there was someone in there too. A little person that Finn and I created together.

"I am sorry though that I was so naive. I should have known more than I did."

Finn growled. "No. You don't get to be sorry. This was entirely my fault because I DO know better. I do know how all this works. I could have used a condom. Told you about pills. But I didn't."

"Why? Did you forget?" I asked.

Finn shook his head. "No, I didn't forget, Say. I've never forgotten since the day I lost my virginity at sixteen. Not one single time."

"I don't understand."

"We belong together, Say. The idea of you pregnant with my kid is...everything. If I'd have known you weren't aware of what could happen, I would have talked to you about it. That's on me. But I still don't regret it. Not one bit."

"So, what you're saying, is that this is all your fault?" I asked, looking up into his handsome face. I reached out and cupped his face in my hand, his stubble scratching the inside of my palm.

Finn laughed and held me tighter. "No. This is nobody's fault. I don't want either of us to think of it that way. If we're having a baby, it's something to celebrate. This is fate. This is *us*."

I exhaled and relaxed against Finn who kissed my forehead. "I love you," I said.

Finn murmured against my hair and his words shot straight through to my very core. "Fiercely. Possessively. Crazily. Always."

Josh came back in record time with a bag of several different brands of pregnancy tests before getting a call about a stranded vehicle and having to leave.

Finn stayed in the bar while I was in the bathroom,

carefully following the instructions on the back of each box.

When I came out of the bathroom, Finn set the timer on the stove for three minutes. He pulled me against him and whispered reassurances against my forehead as we waited. When the timer dinged, he looked down at me. "Do you want me to check?"

I nodded. He was in the bathroom for longer than it would take to glance down and count the lines.

"And?" I called out.

Finally, after what seemed like eons, Finn emerged with a huge smile on his beautiful face. Tears in his blue eyes. He stalked over to me and lifted me up in the air. "Baby?" he asked, planting kisses across my eyelids and down my cheeks.

"Yeah?" I asked, breathlessly.

Finn's smile grew even wider. He looked deeply into my eyes and whispered, "We're having a baby."

"We are?" The happiness warmed my body from the inside out. I was tingling all over.

Finn and I had created life.

Together.

CHAPTER 19

SAWYER

There is something about impending motherhood that creates a shift within you. A shift toward the future. It also brings out the most protective parts of you. I spent every waking moment thinking of how best to protect this baby.

I'd gone to the doctor with Finn shortly after I'd taken all the tests. The doctor confirmed I was more than two and a half months along which means I'd probably gotten pregnant immediately after Finn and I had gotten together. If I'd have found out any later it would have been my belly that would have tipped me off. It was like the second we found out I was pregnant it popped out like the baby got word we knew and it was okay to show people now.

Which reminded me of the other thing impending motherhood changes.

It takes your current patience level and shreds it.

I was on edge like never before.

I was in the library trying to write to ease my mind, but only two words came to me. Protect. Defend.

I wasn't a real poet by any means, but even I knew that two or three words still wasn't enough to string together something that made any sense.

Frustrated with writing, I gave up.

I decided to read the poem *The Caged Bird* by Maya Angelou.

Each time I'd read it in the months I'd been in Outskirts I'd felt either sad or angry or powerful, depending on my mood.

I read it again and again.

Nothing.

I sighed and closed the book. I reached for a rag and began to clean the outside layer of dust from the tattered cover. I might as well get some work done if I couldn't concentrate on anything else.

Maddy was standing guard outside. Since my mother didn't require full-time care anymore, she volunteered to stay with us and help protect us until this business with Richard was over.

If it was ever over.

I really want it to be over.

The bells above the library door chimed, pulling me from my inner thoughts. Maddy peeked her head inside the door. "Josh called, said this one was on his way."

"Thank you," I said, grateful that she decided to stay on with us although I found it odd she still wore her pink smiley face scrubs.

In walked a thickset young man who I'd never seen before. He was in his early thirties and no more than five and a half feet tall. The gleam from the overhead lights shone off his completely hairless head. His clean-shaven cheeks were as round as the rest of him, giving him an additional air of youth. The sleeves of his untucked white shirt were rolled up to his elbows. The collar stained with sweat.

He looked around the room from the walls to the books with a curiosity and wonderment in his eyes. He was adorable in a way I never thought an adult man could be.

I painted a smile on my face to cover the worry. "Hello. We're not quite open just yet. But feel free to look around. Can I help you with something?" I asked.

The man looked at me and instantly smiled, showing off two bright white front teeth that were slightly longer than the rest. His voice was smooth and high-pitched, almost feminine. "Why hello there, cutie-pie. O.M.G. I love your hair. So fierce. I want to scalp you so I can make me a wig out of it." He looked at the confusion I could feel written all over my face. "And yes, that was totally a compliment."

"Thank you?" I responded to this odd yet wonder-fully strange man.

"I am Wilfredo," he said, holding his hand to his chest, bowing at the waist. "My friends call me...Wilfredo."

I couldn't help but chuckle. His personality was huge and took up most of the space in my tiny library. "I'm..."

"Sawyer, I know. Joshy-boo told me. She said you reopened the library so I had to come check it out for myself." He looked around from shelf to shelf, running his hands across the spines of the once dusty books that between Finn and myself were nearly all clean and restored to lendable condition once more. "Bravo, my dear. Well done. This place doesn't look nearly as condemned as it used to."

"Are you from here?" I set down the book of poetry on the table.

Wilfredo nodded. "Born and raised in the mud, but I moved out to California a few years back after meeting the man of my dreams online." He blinked rapidly and looked wistfully into the fluorescent lights overhead.

"Sounds romantic," I commented, finishing wiping off the book and setting it in its usual spot on the shelf.

"Yeah," he sighed dramatically. "It was. Until I got out there and alas, my Justin Bieber look-a-like was a lot less Biebs and a lot more...Lyle Lovett." He scrunched up his nose so I took it as a bad thing.

"That's a shame."

"Not really. I may not have found my dream man, but I fell in love with Cali. Been out there ever since. What about you? Josh says you haven't been here too long. How are you liking our little backward town in the middle of nowhere USA?"

"Actually, I love it here," I said, but the feelings that normally came with that statement were nowhere to be found. "It's home."

"Yeah, I get it. I want to hate this place, I really do. But it really is a great town." Wilfredo pulled out a chair and sat down, fanning himself with a yellow pamphlet. He chuckled. "I mean, if the homo population ever increased from say...one, and by one I do mean THE one, being me, then I'd move back here in a heartbeat. Living with my beautiful ripped swamp-boy in overalls. Watching him de-muck things or pick up heavy things, or whatever it is they do around here that could be sexy if I think about it hard enough." He smiled. "I'd be living my own little gay redneck fantasy. Ah, that would be the life."

I laughed and sat down across from him. "I think I like you, Wilfredo."

"I like you too, Sawyer. So, what's your story? How did you end up in Outskirts?"

"It's a very long story," I said with a sigh.

"Give me the short version of your long story. I've got time. My sister is still at Dr. Maloy's down the road getting her last check-up before the baby is born. That's why I'm back in town. To spoil my new niece and nephew. The newest members of my sister's ever-growing litter of human cubs."

"Congratulations."

"Thank you. Now, back to your story. Short version. Go." He snapped his fingers and closed his eyes.

"Well," I thought for a moment on how to shorten my story and not drag my new friend into the heaviness of my life. I liked having someone new ask me about my relationship with Finn, it reminded me that we were still new. It was like having a secret that only I got to decide how much or how little of us I would share with others.

"I needed a change so when I found out that my mother owned land here I decided that I wanted to come check it out for myself. I took her old camper and truck and I've been here ever since."

"I have a feeling your short version is like the Cliffs-Notes of the CliffsNotes of your story." Wilfredo wiped the sweat beading up on his forehead with a handkerchief from his pocket.

I leaned forward and whispered. "I would say you're right."

"You got yourself a man, Red?" Wilfredo asked. "I know the pickings are slim around here but..." he paused when he saw my hand drop to my burgeoning baby belly.

He gasped. "Spill girl. Who is he?"

"If you're from here then you probably know him," I said, biting my lip. "Finn Hollis?"

Wilfredo's mouth dropped open and his eyes widened. He squealed so loud I had to cover my ears. He then hurriedly made a backward sign of the cross. "Sweet baby Jesus, you bagged the lord of the swamp?"

"Uh, he's. Well, we..."

"He knocked you up. OMG I would KILL for that man to knock me up." He held out his hand, palm side facing me. "No, my sweet red one, not another word. I just need to sit here and let all this sexiness sink in for a moment." He closed his eyes, continuing to fan himself with the paper turned fan in his hand until his phone rang. "That's my sister, I've got to help her back into the car before she tips over." He removed his legs from the table and stood up. "It was nice to meet you, Sawyer, I hope to see you again before I go back to Cali."

"I'd like that very much," I said, and I meant it. Wilfredo brought with him a bright light I wouldn't mind having around more often.

"Are you still working at Critter's?" he asked. "Josh said you guys were helping him out a bit."

"Yeah, sure am. Dinner shift tomorrow if you want to come by."

"I'll be there!" Wilfredo looked down at the paper in his hands like he was just remembering something. He set it down on the table. "Here, I almost forgot, this was in your door when I got here, but I've been using it to fan myself. It's as hot as the bowels of hell in this town. I guess some things never change. See ya, Sexy, Sawyer! Take care of that baybay! See you tomorrow. Save me a place under the Sandy Bennett."

Did he just say what I think he just said?

The bells above the door chimed again. Wilfredo was gone just as quickly as he appeared. Blowing through like a multicolored tumbleweed of fun.

I was rolling around his words in my head when I went to toss the flyer Wilfredo had handed me. I'd just released it into the trash when my heart seized.

It wasn't just a fan or a flyer. It was *the* flyer. The one for God's Light.

A shiver of dread rippled through me. The sharp spike of dread pinched my spine, the one I'd always felt when my father was near.

I covered my mouth in a silent scream as my blood ran cold. My head spun. It wasn't the flyer itself that had me holding onto the table for support. It was the note on the inside, handwritten over the print in thick bright red ink.

Like mother like daughter. -Ezekiel 16:44

CHAPTER 20

SAWYER

After receiving what I knew was a threat from Richard, you'd think I'd have been panicked. Afraid.

I was neither.

In fact, I felt an eerie sense of calm washed over me as I made my way over to Critter's Bar and scanned the thousands of picture frames covering the walls. When I didn't find what I was looking for I dragged out a ladder from the store room and began to read every single ting hanging from the ceiling. It took me an hour before I found what I was looking for. Two tings with strings a little lower than all the others, hanging directly above the big corner table in the back corner by the window.

I HAD a date with Sandy tonight. I think she's the one.

-Bennett

THIS MIGHT GO down as the worst date in history.

-Sandy

NOT KNOWING what I was specifically searching for I stood on my tiptoes and poked my fingers around on the rafters. Sure enough, sitting on the top of the rafter between the two tings was a cell phone. I turned it on and almost fell off the chair at what popped up on the screen.

"What are you doing up there?" Finn asked as he came in the door. He grabbed me by the legs and lifted me off the chair, gently setting me on my feet. "You could hurt yourself."

I held up the phone.

"What is that?" he asked.

Knowing that what I just saw could change everything when it came to Richard, I handed it over to Finn carefully like it was a precious stone although in my eyes it was much more valuable. "I think I just found Sandy Bennett."

IN THE ANIMAL KINGDOM, when a mother feels like her young is in danger, she does whatever it takes to keep them out of harm's way. Even if that something seems ridiculous or illogical to anyone on the outside looking in.

Even if that means sacrificing her own life for theirs.

A giraffe will try to ward off a hungry pack of lions by kicking and attacking.

The usually docile elephant will suddenly and

aggressively charge at a human for getting too close to her baby while it drinks from a stream.

An alligator will carry its young in its mouth for up to a year to keep them safe and make sure they will survive to adulthood at all costs.

A brown bear will raise her cubs near populations of humans, their biggest enemy, to ward off adult male bears who are known to kill cubs who aren't theirs.

Human mothers are very much the same. We are animals after all. Our very nature screams at us to protect at all cost.

Call it hormones.

Call it instinct.

It's nature— written in our very DNA, it surfaces once we become mothers. We will do impossible, sometimes crazy things to keep our children safe.

But what those on the outside don't understand is sometimes that kind of protection comes with a whole lot of crazy. Because if crazy is what it takes to protect my child.

Then so be it.

The threat written on that flyer was my breaking point, setting off within me my basic instinct to protect.

I could no longer sit idly by and wait for something to happen. I couldn't stand like the giraffe in an open field with those I love and wait to be circled and pounced on by the hungry lions.

No, I couldn't, not anymore.

Which was why this giraffe was headed straight into the lion's den.

CHAPTER 21

FINN

I was going to be a father. I was already so in love with a child that I'd never even met yet because it was mine. I couldn't imagine ever turning on that child. On Sawyer.

Family was all that mattered in the world.

Family was also why I was standing there on the Brillhart County Fairgrounds under the elaborate church tent. Today was Sawyer's idea. One I was against. One I was still against.

Not because it was a bad idea, but because it went against my greater need to want to toss her over my shoulder and carry her back to our cave where I knew I could keep her safe.

There I was, standing beside an open tent flap, looking right at the man we'd all spent way too much time fearing. Hating. I couldn't say that I was nervous. It was more like I was nervous for him. He was only a few feet away. All it would take was a close of the flap and then I'd reach across the desk and wrap my bare hands around his—

"Can I help you?" Richard asked, acknowledging my presence. He looked up from his desk and much to my surprise he appeared to be...average at best. Brown hair. Brown eyes. The standard issue glasses from the eighties. Medium-sized plain black frames. He was also shorter than I thought he would be. Much smaller than the huge persona that preceded him. I imagined him to be huge. Muscular. Menacing. This guy was five foot nine at best. He wasn't a large man. I would even go so far as to call him skinny and shapeless.

But this was no average man.

This man had laid hands on Sawyer.

He'd hurt her. Threatened her.

My blood began to boil. I flexed my fingers so I wouldn't ball of my fists and send them flying into the man's face. That wasn't part of the plan.

Unfortunately.

"Yes, I think you can... help me," I finally answered in the friendliest voice I could muster. "I wanted to know more about the church. I saw your flyers."

"We're getting ready to start the service but what would you like to know?" he asked. "Do you currently belong to a church?"

I shook my head and looked around the office space that looked more corporate and less Christian, especially for being in a tent. "No, I don't. Unless you consider being dragged to Easter and Christmas Mass by my parents every year as a kid, belonging to a church."

"I do not," Richard said sternly, taking off his

reading glasses and polishing them on the sleeve of his white button-down.

Richard gave me a quick once-over with his beady little eyes. I could see my dismissal written all over his face. He put his glasses back on and picked up a pen, dropping his head back down to his work. "Service is three times a day. The times are posted on the board outside my office. There are some flyers as well if you'd like to take one. We are only here for the summer but we have a housing unit in North Carolina where our main church is located if you wanted to come back with us and see what it's all about."

That was his pitch? The church was his entire life and THAT was his pitch? Miller could have done a better job.

"I already have a flyer," I said, waving around the yellow piece of paper in my hand. "But you see, I need more than just the service. I've been feeling a little lost lately. I'm looking for some real-life guidance through God."

"How so?" Richard asked, sounding annoyed. He kept checking his watch for the time. He never asked me to take a seat.

"I recently lost someone close to me. Actually, it wasn't recently. It was a couple of years ago. But, I can't seem to move on. When I heard you were coming to town, I sought you out. I need to know God's plan for me."

Richard shook his head. "We all need God son. If you'd like, you can sign up for counseling with Pastor Maryn. He's over by the tent setting up for the afternoon. He'll be more than happy to help you," Richard said, holding his hand out to the flap, furthering my dismissal. "I look forward to seeing you at the service."

Shit.

It wasn't going how I'd expected it to go. The safety of my entire world was at stake. I needed to keep him in here for as long as possible. At least for another few minutes or so.

Time for Plan B.

I was nervous. Damned near desperate when I turned back toward Richard. "I'm sorry I took up your time. It's just that I have a lot of time of my own on my hands now that my land holdings company has a new management team. I've got nothing but time to think and money to spend, but no one to spend it on anymore. It all seems cheap. Cars, houses, things. I'd much rather spend money on things that matter. Like my soul." I pushed open the door. "Does Pastor Maryn also handle the donations? Never mind. I'll talk to him myself. I see that you're busy. Have a good afternoon, sir."

"Son, why don't you come back and sit a while," Richard called out.

I stifled a laugh before turning back around.

"Sorry, I was so distracted before," Richard said, pushing his papers to the side. "How about you talk and I'll listen. Then, maybe we will see if God can direct us to his grand plan for you."

Richard gestured to the chair in front of the desk the same way he'd gestured to the door only seconds before.

I took a seat. "Thank you. I really appreciate this," I said as genuinely as I could although the words *Imma kill you, motherfucker* was what was really running through my head.

"Tell me again. Why do you have all this time on your hands?" Richard asked, resting his elbows on the desk, his index fingers pressed together in the shape of a steeple.

It was almost too easy. Money. He wanted to talk about my money.

I spent a while spewing bullshit to him. For the most part, he listened and nodded. Occasionally he'd recite something from the Bible I knew didn't mean what he thought it meant. Just because I didn't choose religion didn't mean I was ignorant of it. After a while he asked me about my family.

"My parents moved away a while ago. I don't see them much anymore. We don't really get along well."

One of many lies I told him that afternoon. It hurt me to lie about them when I don't think there was a time I'd ever thought bad about my parents. I don't think they missed a single one of my baseball games or practices. They were there. Physically and emotionally. Parents-wise, I hit the lottery.

I stared at Richard.

Others weren't as lucky.

"Why didn't you get along with your parents, son. Next to God, family is what's most important."

Bullshit.

"I can't really pinpoint where it all went wrong," I started, dropping my head into my hands for a bit of dramatic effect and mentally thanking Mrs. Doogan, my high school guidance counselor, for convincing me to take that semester of drama as one of my electives. I lifted my head. "Do you have a family, Pastor?"

Richard nodded. "I'm a widower, but I have a daughter."

"I'm sorry about your wife," I offered.

Even though she's ALIVE. Which I was hoping he had no idea about.

"We all have our fair share of problems, son. My wife and I weren't always on the same page. My daughter is going through a rebellious phase. Even with my guidance, she's lost her way."

"Again, I'm sorry to hear that."

Richard waved me off. "Don't apologize. I'm very, very certain that she'll find her way back to us soon." He crossed a leg over his knee. "One way or another."

Like hell she will.

"And if she doesn't?" I asked.

"That's not an option," Richard said in a very serious tone, looking down at his hands. "Defiance is never an option." He cleared his throat and looked back up at me and smiled. "Not when it comes to God."

Richard stood up and walked behind me. He peered out the plastic tent window then lowered the flap for the shade casting the room in a muted light. "I have a service in a few moments. One of our very last for the summer. I'm sorry I can't give you more time. But tell me this. Do your real problems lie with your relationship with your family or your relationship with God? Or…" he walked back around the desk and leaned over it with his hands flat on the top. His eyebrows pointed inward. A twisted cruel smile pulled at his lips. "Or…is it a woman who has you seeking out HIS holy plan?"

"Well," I started, about to spew some more bullshit about a made-up problem when he interrupted me.

His voice took on an entirely different tone. This time it was low. Bitter. "Because I think the real problem might stem from your sins. Specifically, your fornication...with my *daughter*."

I almost laughed. "They said you knew everything. I'm surprised it took you this long to figure out who I was."

Just then the feedback of a microphone pierced through the speakers in the big tent next door. Sawyer's voice was coming through loud and clear.

I smiled up at Richard who stood straight and appeared confused as he darted for the door. I stood in front of him, blocking his way. "Actually, fornication with your daughter isn't a problem at all. Considering she's not *your* daughter."

Richard fumed as he marched passed me into the big tent but came to a halt when he saw Sawyer standing at the front of the room addressing the huge crowd that had gathered for the service.

She held up the 'Sandy Bennett' cell phone.

He was just in time.

CHAPTER 22

SAWYER

There's a certain amount of fear that comes with any kind of public speaking. Yet, as I walk down the aisle under the tent, surrounded by the kind people that were in my daily life for twenty-one years. I felt no fear.

None. Maybe because this was what was familiar to me for so long.

My palms were dry. My breaths were even.

I felt powerful. Strong.

And ready to face my demons head-on.

Maybe because my child growing in my stomach was giving me a new sense of bravery I've never known before. Maybe because I was about to say words that I've wanted to say for so long to so many that my excitement outweighed my fear.

Critter, Maddy, and Miller were manning the entrances and exits. Josh stood next to me in her police uniform looking every bit the part of the angry cop. Her job was to also make sure that I was not interrupted until I had said all I had to say.

The tent was full. Every available seat had a body in it.

When we reached the podium, Josh leaned over and grabbed the microphone. "Ladies and gentlemen," she said, "we have a quick public safety presentation for you before your service starts today. We apologize for the interruption. Please listen carefully and we will be out of your way as soon as possible. Thank you."

Josh nodded to me. It was my turn.

I looked over a sea of faces. Some familiar. Some not.

"My name is Sawyer Dixon," I started. However, I paused when I saw my father standing in the back corner of the tent staring at me like he'd seen a ghost. I didn't think I'd be able to find the words to continue because my heart was beating so loud I didn't know if I could hear my own voice.

As I began to speak, Richard pushed his way down the aisle Josh met him in the middle and shook her head blocking him from going any further.

"Like a lot of you, I grew up in this church. Just like my mother. Every single day of my life lived in fear. Fear that my *father* would kill my mother. I feared that he would kill me. I feared that he *wouldn't* kill us and we would have to keep on living these torturous lives forever. He repeatedly beat, raped, and starved my mother, to the point where she couldn't go on and decided to kill herself." I took a deep calming breath.

"And, for a while, I was so mad. I didn't know why I was so mad until I realized I wasn't mad at her at all. I was jealous. Jealous that she found a way out and I was still there.

"I was now the one being beaten and told it was discipline. I was threatened and told it was God's word or God's plan. I was deprived of love because in this church a woman, a girl, we are deemed unworthy of love. We are starved affection. We are so beneath the men that we can't eat at the same table or make eye contact. Yet, my father continued to preach family first while sucking the life force from us with each passing second."

"Liar! You have no proof!" my father called out, shaking his closed fist in the air.

"Simmer down," Josh warned. Placing her hand on her gun holster. "She's getting to that part."

The audience began to speak to one another in hushed whispers. My eyes fell on a young woman in the audience standing in the back.

Bridget.

I gave her a smile and she looked as though I was on a suicide mission.

I straightened my shoulders and glanced over to Finn, then Miller, and then finally my real father.

Critter.

Who looked angry yet proud from where he stood on the opposite end of the tent from Richard.

It felt good to have him witness this. It felt good to be up there saying the things that I'd been thinking needed to be said my entire life.

"Someone told me recently that it doesn't matter what your religion believes in regardless of how silly or stupid it may seem to others. What matters is what you take from it. How it makes you feel. Nothing about Richard or this church has ever made me feel better or loved or wiser. Or kinder. Under the pretense of love Richard teaches hate."

"All lies. Don't listen to her. She's a deflector. She left the church. This is the devil's work. All of it!" Richard yelled. His face turning red with his anger. And just like he'd always done with me...

I dismissed him.

In my heart. In my mind.

In my life.

He was not important enough to acknowledge. To look me in the eye.

So, I moved on.

"I'm not going to tell you again," Josh warned, moving to stand right in front of Richard.

"I've never come forward before because I had no proof, nothing to back up what I'm telling you today." I grabbed the cell phone from my back pocket and looked to Miller in the back of the room who gave me the nod to go ahead.

"But I left and found a new home. A new family. Things have changed." I thought about the child growing in my belly. "Everything has changed."

The crowd again began to speak to one another in hushed whispers.

I pressed play on the phone.

The light from the projector Miller had installed the night before came to life on the tent wall behind me. The audience gasped as the first clip from the phone showed Bridget's own husband pushing her head into the dining room table while yelling at her for accidentally making eye contact. The second clip was of Richard and it looked as if it was taken through the window of our house on the second story. Richard was straddling my mother on their bed. It was hard to watch. I felt helpless then and watching it now made me feel just as helpless.

I turned around to face the crowd to gauge the reactions instead of watching the video. Most of them had their eyes locked on the screen, flinching with the women on the wrong end of wrath.

Clip after clip showed high ranking members of the church all doing much the same. When the video was over, Josh already had Richard in cuffs and was leading him away. He screamed over his shoulder, "The devil has won this round but God WILL prevail in the end."

"That's the thing," I said. "All of this was done under the guise of God and discipline. I don't know what kind of God would look at these videos and think that is properly represented his will. And if that's the kind of god you choose to believe in, it's not a god I want to know."

"I'm proud of you," Finn said, leading me away and underneath the tent flap behind the podium, the opposite direction of the crowd.

As soon as we were on the other side, someone stepped into our path. I took a startled step back. Finn pushed me behind his body. His entire body stiffened as he readied himself to go on the offense.

"It's just me. Bridget." I peeked out from around Finn and he stepped aside. I approached her like I would a small child who might easily scare.

"Thank you for leaving us that phone."

Bridget kicked at the dirt. "No, thank you for using it. I stole it years ago. Been sneaking around taking videos here and there. Never really knew what I was going to do with them or how I was going to get people to see them. It's me who should be thanking you."

"Do you need a place to go, Bridget?" Finn asked using the same soft tone I was.

She shook her head. "My husband was carted off as well. I think I'm gonna be okay. Gonna go back to North Carolina and ransack the house. Take anything of value and I'm going to take a page from your book and… escape."

There was an excitement. A life in her voice that hadn't been there before. Bridget skipped off as my heart skipped while watching her leave.

"Look what you did, baby," Finn said, pulling me into the crook of his arm. "She's going to have her own life now. A real life all because of you."

I was on the verge of tears. I couldn't believe it. "No." I shook my head. "Not because of me. Because of *her*."

"You're right," Finn agreed. "I think Bridget was much stronger than we gave her credit for."

Bridget had proven to be more than I'd judged her to be. I'd never make that same mistake again. Because, as we'd just witnessed, Bridget was a force to be reckoned with.

And the day of reckoning was here.

CHAPTER 23

SAWYER

Because of the serious nature of Richard's crimes, he was denied bail. He was awaiting trial in the Brillhart County prison. We were told the evidence was ironclad and he wouldn't be seeing freedom for a very long time.

If ever.

I didn't know if I could ever get used to not having to look over my shoulder, although my steps felt a bit lighter and the mood between those I care about most had improved considerably.

Finn told me to meet him at the library. Of course, we happened to be getting a hurricane that very night. My first one.

When I had asked Miller how I needed to prepare for the hurricane he laughed and told me, "It's only a category one. You only need to buy some more beer."

"What do you do for category five?" I'd asked.

Josh answered by telling me that the best way to

prepare for category five was to place your head between your knees and kiss your ass goodbye.

I'd make sure to remember that.

I arrived at the library right on time. "What is all this?" I asked, looking around the dark room. The only light was coming from an overhead projector. Finn stood in the back of the room, fiddling with dials on multiple little black boxes. "Finn?"

Finn guided me by the hand to the center of the room where he'd pushed aside all the desks and set up a blanket and pillows all over the floor. "You can call me Professor Hollis, and tonight you are my pupil, so have a seat young lady." He moved to the front of the room and stood in front of a large screen hanging from the ceiling.

"What's going on? What is this?" I asked, perching myself among the soft pillows. "I thought we were here because of the hurricane, but the storm isn't set to come in until later tonight."

"You are correct. We are here because it's the highest point in town and the furthest away from the water in case of flooding. But I thought we could get here early. I wanted to spend some time educating that precious and very sexy mind of yours in the ways of our odd world. All in the name of your quest for knowledge, I wanted to teach you some things before the power goes out."

"Okay," I said, skeptically, folding my legs up like a pretzel.

Finn smiled and that dimple I love so much appeared. "Welcome to an extremely shortened version of everything in our world. My name is Professor Hollis and I will be in charge of molding your mind this evening," Finn said, dramatically extending his arms.

I laughed at how seriously he was taking this and I was touched at how much trouble he'd gone through.

"Shall we begin?" Finn pushed up the fake plastic black-rimmed glasses up the bridge of his nose. He was wearing a long white lab coat. He had a remote in his hand and he stood off to the side of the projector. He clicked a button and a black and white picture of an ape appeared on the screen. "You'll note the pen and pad on the floor in front of you, Miss Dixon. I recommend taking notes so you won't fall behind before the test."

I picked up the notebook and pen and nodded for Finn to continue. "Very good. First lesson. Evolution." He clicked the remote. On the screen was written the very next words he spoke. "People came from apes."

He clicked the remote again. It was a drawing. A portrait of a man wearing a white wig with the American Flag across the background. "Lesson two. American Politics."

He shook his head and clicked through two more slides. "All you need to know is that modern politics aren't rooted in any sort of factual realm created by humans." He clicked the remote again and a picture of a group of twenty-something adults were sitting on a couch in a cafe. "Now, on to pop culture. How much do you know about the show 'Friends'?"

"Not a thing."

"Good, because this is where I take over Professor Hollis." Miller showed up wearing a matching lab coat and plastic-rimmed glasses. He took the remote from

Finn and they exchanged long hard handshakes and pseudo stern looks.

"I didn't even hear you come in!" I said to Miller as Finn joined me on the floor.

He buffed his nails on his coat. "I mean. Most people don't. I AM a distant relative to Batman. Which brings me to our next subject." He clicked the remote and the screen showed dozens of illustrations of men and women all dressed in tight-fitting costumes and masks. I recognized some of them and others I didn't. "Super-heroes and all the ways they are incredibly awesome," Miller said.

I laughed through the entire next hour where Miller's lessons ranged from 'Why Nickelback's music doesn't suck all that bad,' and 'Why Bruce Willis should be nominated for Sainthood.'

I leaned against Finn and laughed as Miller went off and tangent after tangent. While he gave his lesson, Josh, Critter, Wilfredo, and even my mother had arrived with coolers and other supplies in hand. When my mother grew tired Critter led her to the back room where he'd set up a cot for her to rest on.

"And the very last lesson plan I have for you today folks is..." Miller clicked the remote, and a bird and a bee appeared on the screen. "The birds and the bees. Now when a man and woman love each other very much they," he made a sign with his hands. His index finger poking in and out of a hole he created with his other hand. I laughed when I finally got what he was indicating. I laughed so hard my sides started to hurt. "They do that. And then, the man's baby seed lassoes the woman's baby egg-thing and BOOM. That's how babies are made and if you're really, really lucky and you find the right person?" Miller grinned at Josh. "They'll even make you a sandwich after."

"Boooooo!" Josh and Wilfredo shouted, throwing candy wrappers at Miller who ducked and dodged the assault.

"Detention for you both!" Miller shouted.

Critter, who was seated at a table nearby was rolling his eyes but he was smiling. "Did you skip that day in school, son?"

Miller shrugged. "Actually, I received an attendance award in high school."

"That wasn't an attendance award," Finn laughed. "That was a warning to your parents that if you skipped any more school, you'd be expelled because you'd missed more classes than any other student."

"And? What part of that doesn't scream attendance award?" Miller grabbed a beer and Josh rolled her eyes.

"You just wait until your boobs are fat and your belly is all round with my baby," he murmured pulling her in for a kiss.

"My luck I'd just be puking my guts out and feeling like shit for nine months," Josh said, pushing him away.

"I bet you'd look hot doing all that puking." Miller wagged his eyebrows.

"You're gross," Josh chided, but she didn't push him away this time when he went in and kissed her on the tip of her nose.

"Speaking of feeling ill," I said, holding my stomach as the smell of whatever candy Josh had just unwrapped was about to cause my lunch to come back up. I read that occasional sickness was common but this was a lot more than occasional.

"Are you okay?" Finn asked, growing concern written on his face. "This little one giving you a hard time?"

"I'm fine. Just a little he or she probably has really long legs like his father."

"I wish I could knock someone up," Wilfredo said on a sigh, leaning in so far into one of the coolers that his head disappeared.

"Uh, you can knock someone up. You're a dude. Presumably a dude with a dick," Miller argued.

"Yeah, but unless gay sex suddenly requires the pill then it's never gonna happen. At least not in the biblical sense. Because although these creatures are phenomenal and fierce and I want to be them." He pointed to us, rolling his index finger in a small circle and grimacing. "What they got going on below the belt scares the ever-loving shit out of me."

Miller stared at Josh and slowly nodded. "You and me both, man." He shook his head. "You and me both."

"Thank you for all of this," I said, placing a kiss on Finn's lips.

"Thank you," Finn said. My heart fluttered.

"For what? I didn't do anything." I chuckled.

Finn placed his hand on my belly. "You're doing everything."

"What do you mean you only packed three cases of beer. It's a hurricane! I don't think I can ever forgive you!" Miller yelled at Wilfredo who remained calm and produced a bottle of vodka from his backpack.

"Shots?" Wilfredo asked, shaking the bottle.

Miller snatched it from his hands. "Forgiven."

"Don't forget I owe you an ass kicking for knocking up my daughter," Critter said, narrowing his eyes at Finn.

"Oh, I didn't forget," Finn said. "I'd expect nothing less."

Critter nodded. "Good. We're on the same page then."

Sometimes, I didn't know whether they were joking or not. But I thought it best to stay out of it and let them do whatever it is they needed to do to prove who was manlier.

"I'm going to go check on my mother," I said. Finn helped me to a standing position and I carefully stepped over the pillows on the floor and navigated around my friends and family, heading toward the back room.

Miller was chugging from the vodka bottle, clear liquid spilling down his chin onto his black t-shirt.

"I think I might want to try my chances with the hurricane," Josh muttered as I passed her by.

I slowly opened the door to the back-storage area and went inside, shutting it behind me so that Miller's loud voice wouldn't wake my mother if she was sleeping. I tiptoed toward the cot only to find it empty.

I quickly scanned the rest of the room and I didn't see her. Something felt off, like there was a shift in the air I couldn't explain. It felt thicker. Heavier.

"Mother?" I looked into the dark corner where I was keeping some books that needed to be shipped off to have the spines repaired. I saw movement. "There you are," I exhaled in relief. "You scared me. What are you doing back there? All the newer books are on the shelves in the main room. Anything in particular you're looking for?" I kneeled down to tie my shoelace which I'd just notice had come undone when I heard footsteps.

Heavy footsteps.

Not my mother's footsteps.

"Yes. YOU," answered a deep throaty male voice.

I froze for a moment then realized if I was going to escape this time I was going to have to act fast. I made a leap toward the door but I wasn't quick enough. A large hand came around my chest and another covered my nose and mouth to muffle my scream before it even had a chance to leave my lips.

"Shhhh, I have your whore of a mother, and it's up to you whether she remains alive or not," Richard whispered bitterly into my ear. He smelled just as I remembered. Like whiskey and arrogance. "I locked all of the doors of this building from the outside. If you so much as try and draw attention to yourself, even one little squeak of a noise, I'll set this entire place ablaze with every single of those heathens trapped inside." He showed me a metal lighter, flicking it open and setting the flame too high so I could see he was serious about carrying through with his threat.

I felt helpless. Panicked.

My heart was beating rapidly and all I could think about was protecting Finn and my baby.

There was nothing I could do but comply. And as he dragged me out into the night I thought he tripped over something but I was wrong. He'd kicked over something. That something was a gas can.

With a flick of his wrist, he sent the lighter and the

tiny flame cascading into the gas can, causing it to immediately erupt in a fire ball which was anything but tiny.

I tried to get to them. To move my limbs but they wouldn't cooperate. I was breathing erratically, taking in more and more of whatever he had pressed into his palm covering my nose and mouth.

I felt nauseated. The sound of Richard's callous laugh surrounded me as he dragged me further and further away from the library. The storm hadn't yet brought the rain but the wind spread the flames quickly and just as my vision started to blur I managed to make out the last sight I ever wanted to see.

The roof of the library caved in...and collapsed.

CHAPTER 24

FINN

It all happened so quickly. It sounded like an explosion then the roof of the storage room was collapsing.

Sawyer.

I raced toward the storage room with Critter while Miller attempted to open the front door which turned out to be locked from the outside. Together, Josh and Miller managed to ram through it just enough to get everyone out. The pouring rain had doused the fire.

Critter and I, with burning palms, had pushed aside the fallen roof, frantically searching for Sawyer and Caroline.

It wasn't until we'd moved the last fallen beam we'd realized…they weren't there. I breathed out a sigh of relief only to have a sharp stab of fear spike through me like a lightning bolt to the chest.

I glanced over to Critter who kicked over some debris with an angry roar. "No! Not again, no!" he yelled pulling at his hair.

I balled my fists and tried to breathe through my nose to calm my racing heart.

It looked as if Critter and I we were on the same page, and that page only had one word written on it.

Richard.

CHAPTER 25

SAWYER

All I heard was crickets. The wind slapped wet leaves and mud against my face. It was raining lightly but the wind was blowing so hard each drop of water stung against my skin. It smelled like sulfur and decay.

I tried to peel my eyes open, but they wouldn't comply. I was sitting in a few inches of water. My shorts were completely soaked through.

Finn.

My family. My friends.

The library. The roof collapsing.

It sobered me up and pulled me from the haze I was in. I jolted awake. My eyes sprung open, only to find myself bound at the wrists behind a tree at my back in the swamp.

I was terrified that I lost all the people that meant most me the world. The only thing that kept me from shaking uncontrollably with fear—the only thing that kept me sucking in my next breath, was the life growing inside of me.

I felt sick to my stomach. Everything ached. My body sat heavy upon my bones as if I were carrying around another pile of flesh and muscle on the outside of mine. Like gravity was working overtime to pull me into the center of the earth.

It was difficult to lift my arms. My eyes wouldn't open fully and I was forced to peer out into the darkness of this world through tiny slits. It must have been the effects of whatever it was that Richard had sedated me with.

Everything hurt. My body, my heart, my spirit.

Then I heard a voice and at first, I thought I was imagining things, but her voice was not only clear, but it was also calm.

And it belonged to my mother.

"When you were growing up I saw so much of myself reflected in your eyes. It scared me. A part of me wished you were complacent. Obedient. A person who stood in line and waited their turn and did what they were told and were happy that way. But occasionally I caught a glimpse of fire in your eyes. I recognized the rebellion in you. I knew you had questions bigger than the answers the church would ever give you. Your eyes give you away, Sawyer. They always have. They told me you were no more meant for that life than I was. I was scared for you, but an even bigger part of me was proud, relieved.

I knew you couldn't stay there. That fire in you along with Richard's controlling and abusive ways...it was never going to end well." She pressed her lips together and looked up at the sky. "I was always surprised you hadn't run away earlier. And disappointed in a way."

"I couldn't leave you," I argued. "I could never leave you."

She shook her head. "Which makes it worse. You should have."

"No. Besides, you said if I did that Richard threatened to kill you."

My mother nodded. "He would have. But none of that mattered. You were all that mattered. You are all that matters now."

I dropped my eyes to my stomach. "No. I'm not all that matters now."

My chest tightened at the look of pain on my mother's face. I resolved to stay strong for her. To push the turmoil inside of me down and be there for both my child and my mother.

"I failed you," she said, the wind sent her words barreling toward me, hitting me right in the gut.

"You didn't! You were put in a situation no one could ever imagine themselves in. I couldn't begin to imagine having to make the choices you were faced with. I understand now. I understand why you did everything and I'm the one who's sorry. For ever doubting you. And besides, you're right. We are a lot alike."

"Maybe. Did I ever tell you the story of how you got your name?" My mother asked. She was trying to distract me from the rising water. I needed it because the endless tugging on my restraints was getting me nowhere.

The water was rising quicker and quicker. It was only a matter of time before it was over our heads.

"No," I said, shaking my head. "Tell me." My blood was pumping furiously through me. I felt hyperaware of my surroundings. Of my body. I was tense like I'd never felt before.

In addition to being completely and utterly terrified.

My mother managed a strained chuckle. "Richard wanted to name you Mara. The biblical meaning being bitter or bitterness. It was like everything he did to you was a punishment for my sins against him and he wanted your name to be no different."

"Sounds about right," I muttered, rubbing whatever was tying my hands together and against the bark of the tree to try to slice the bindings apart.

My mother looked to the sky like she could see the story she was telling me unfolding above her. "When Critter and I first got together we would lay out in his sunflower fields for hours watching the sun set and just listening to the leaves rustle around us. We'd talk and drink wine and get sunburnt on our noses." She sighed as she remembered happier times then broke out into a coughing fit.

"Mom! Mom, are you okay?" I called out, hating feeling so helpless.

She nodded. When she regained herself, I blew out a breath of relief.

She continued. "You already know part of the story. But one day there was this little towheaded boy. No more than six or seven years old. I watched him drive his big wheel into the field and with his little rusted pocket knife, he snipped off a flower, waved to Critter, and drove away." She laughed softly. "When I asked Critter about it he told me that the boy did that almost every week. When I asked what he was doing with the flowers, Critter told me that he found the boy in his field one day and he was upset because he was in trouble with his mother for swearing." She shook her head like she still couldn't believe it herself.

"Critter snipped a flower and gave it to the boy. He told him to go and apologize to his mother and give her the flower. Well, it must have worked because every week after that Critter said the boy was there with his own knife snipping away. One for his teacher because he told her that math was for people who didn't have calculators. Another for the lady at the bakery for knocking over her cake display in the window that had taken her all weekend to put together."

"That's kind of adorable," I commented, my heart breaking as my mind replayed the roof collapsing in the library over and over again. Maybe we would have a boy who liked Finn. Maybe he'd never get to meet his father.

While I was breaking inside, Mother spoke as if we were on the porch drinking tea.

"It was adorable. Turns out, it happened so often that they came to deal where Critter roped off a patch of sunflowers just for the boy to take as he pleased."

The rising water was now soaking my shorts up my thighs. I knew had to move faster if I any chance and cutting through my restraints.

My mother looked over at me. She raised her voice above the wind which had picked up. "You were named Sawyer because of Finn." She sighed happily as if we are about to go pick out bridesmaid's dresses and weren't about to meet our ends in a murky swamp.

My stomach felt rock hard. I wanted to flee from this nightmare. I held back the scream that threatened to tear from my throat. "Mother, why aren't you panicking?" I managed to ask, swallowing down my fear in one hard gulp.

She smiled over at me. "I'm terrified for you and the life you and your child may never get to live. But me? I came to terms with my own death years ago."

My mother kept talking. I kept trying to free myself. "Critter and I even joked how if we ever had a girl that she could marry Finn because he already knew what most men would never learn, how to apologize."

Now it was my eyes tearing up as I imagined a little version of Finn causing problems all around Outskirts and fixing them with a flower and a sly dimpled smile. "How did you get Richard to ever agree to the name?"

She looks almost proud when she gave me her answer. "Sawyer means woodcutter in Celtic. All I did was stretch the truth a little. And since I couldn't flat out recommend the name to him because he'd just swat it down, I told some of the ladies in church, but I told them that Sawyer meant carpenter, like the occupation of Jesus himself. Sure enough, before I was about to give birth to you, the name had made its way to Richard. One day he announced to me that your name was going to be Sawyer, like it had been handed down to him in a vision from God himself." She began to laugh hysterically.

"That was very sneaky of you, Mother. I didn't know you had it in you."

She sighed heavily. "I did." Her eyes became unfocused and suddenly it was like she was staring through me and not seeing me. Her head began to make an orbiting motion, small circles.

"Mom?" I yelled.

No response.

"Mom!" I called out louder.

Her eyes closed and she blinked rapidly like she was trying to clear her mind. "Sawyer?" she asked, and then her eyes closed and her chin fell to her chest revealing an angry looking bloody wound on the top of her head. She needed help.

Soon.

"Stay with me, Mom," I called over to her. The water was now above our waists and still rising.

Her eyes remained closed, but she spoke again, only she sounded like she was far away instead of right in front of me. "Mom," she said. "I... I like it when you call me that. It's much better than *Mother*."

Then silence.

"Mom, Mom!" I yelled. Hoping for at the very least another incoherent answer.

Still no answer.

"Moooooom!" I groaned as the water rose and was now at chest level. If my mother stayed in her current position, she'd be breathing in the murky water within the next few minutes. "You need to pick your head up, Mom. Pick it up!" My yells turn into screams.

I pulled at the restraints tying my hands together and growled when they didn't give yet again.

I needed to stay calm. Think. Clear my mind.

With the water rising all around us and the fear of

losing my mother and my unborn child's lives, I harnessed my panic and attempted to find some clarity amongst the chaos.

I'd grown up in a home where the religion was strict and the enforcement of both God and my father's laws were even stricter. I'd bowed my head thousands of times and recited words of faith because I was told they needed to be said. But I'd never truly prayed. I never put any meaning behind the words I was saying. I never believed them enough to be true or had the kind of faith that others found easy to trust in blindly.

Dear God, Universe, Ma'am, Sir, Flying Spaghetti Monster,

I don't know how to pray anymore. Actually, I don't think I ever did. I was taught to always give you thanks and never ask for anything because you would provide me with every-thing I needed and to ask for more would be questioning your will.

A sin.

But since so much has been a lie, I'm going to go out on a limb and assume that asking you for something I need, not want, is okay. Maybe just this once.

I'd start by saying thank you for all you've given me but there isn't any time. I'm going to jump right in and offer you a bargain. Maybe it's wrong, but I don't want to ask you for something so big without offering you something in return.

But I have to try because I don't just have something to lose.

I have everything to lose.

Please, I beg you, spare my mother, she's been through so much. She's endured the unthinkable. She deserves a chance to live her bliss. To be happy. I want her to know how it feels to live without fear and be loved unconditionally by someone who doesn't expect anything in return. And for your generosity in sparing her, I offer you me. But only after the baby is born and safe in her father's arms. Then I'll go with you. Willingly and happily the second I know they are all safe and together.

Please let my family live and I'll do anything you want.

Anything at all.

I repeated my prayer over and over again and at some point, I must have drifted off to sleep because I was dreaming of a blonde woman with a bright smile and a purple silk scarf wrapped around her neck walking toward me. But her feet weren't touching the water, she was walking on top of it. Maybe I was just hallucinating. Or maybe I was already dead. I felt the panic. The very real panic shoot through my veins like a jolt of adrenaline.

If I was dead. It meant the baby was dead too.

"No! I can't be dead. I can't be dead."

The woman crouched before me and smiled. Her white pants and blouse were unwrinkled, unstained. She smelled like fresh linen. She looked familiar, but I couldn't place her. "Don't you worry. You're not dead. Not yet anyway. Your baby is safe, but you have to listen to me very carefully."

"Are you...God?"

The woman laughed and it sounded light and bright. Angelic. "Oh, darlin', they wouldn't want me running things. It would be like a two for one happy hour twenty-four hours a day, seven days a week. It would be a lot more college frat and a lot less holy after-life. You catch my drift?"

"I think so," I answered. "Who are you then?"

She clapped her hands together. "I'm someone who is here to help."

"How?"

The woman thought for a moment, tapping a perfectly polished fingernail against her chin. "You know how when a bad situation comes up people tend to tell you to always look ahead and never look behind you, or something like that."

"Sure, my mother used to say that all the time."

"Well, I'm here to tell you that it's all bullshit. It's what's behind you that counts. It's what's behind you that is going to save you. Don't wait for your knight in shining armor to rescue you, as hot as they can be sometimes. BE your own knight. Rescue yourself. Finn might have rescued your heart, but the rest is up to you now."

As fast as she appeared and before I could ask her what exactly she meant, the woman in white was gone.

I opened my eyes and felt the water at my chin. Water was now splashing up into my eyes. I squinted over at my mother whose face was now only inches away from the rising water. I wished my dream were somehow real and what was behind me was really going to save me. The only thing behind me was the tree I was tied to and countless swamp animals waiting for me to shift from life to death so they could have at my carcass.

I wouldn't give up.

I will never give up.

I felt a new resolve growing within me. A new kind of power, bravery. It was exactly what I needed to push on.

In a last attempt to free my hands I stretched my fingers under the water, searching for anything that I could use as a knife to cut through the rope. The water was flowing around us more like a river than a swamp so it was possible things underneath had shifted.

I touched something hard with my finger where moments ago there was nothing. It was at least six inches and broken or jagged at one end. I didn't know if it was a pipe or broken piece of wood or rock, but I hoped it would do. I maneuvered it between the ropes and started sawing. I dropped it once and then once again before I could do any real damage to the rope. I growled out my frustrations into the rising water that had now reached my mouth. My thoughts were scrambled as I pressed my lips together tightly.

I didn't dare look over to my mother knowing full well she had to be submerged by now. I couldn't let anything distract me from the task at hand.

Both of our lives depended on it.

I had to hurry, but I knew rushing wouldn't get me anywhere. I hummed the lullaby my mother used to sing to me during storms to ease my fears. And as my mind drifted over those times she gave me comfort when she had none of her own, I sawed away.

I took my last large gulp of air right as the water rose over my mouth and then my nose.

After reciting three verses of the lullaby in my head my lungs were burning like they were on fire. With one last push of the restraints against the object, and one last underwater scream, something snapped and my hands broke free.

I emerged from the water, gasping for my first full

breath of air in what seemed like forever. As my lungs took their fill it was as if everything stood still. The splash of each raindrop in the water. The leaves falling from the wind rustled trees. I could see everything now. Everything smelled stronger. Sounded louder. Appeared clearer.

My mind completely cleared. I felt calm. Peaceful.

It was as if I'd been baptized in the dirty water. Christened by the hurricane itself and delivered into the swamp reborn.

I was no longer Sawyer, the girl running from her past. I was Sawyer, the girl from The Outskirts.

A true outlier just like the rest of them.

I remember reading an article for my religious study where a pastor from Alabama said that when God takes you into troubled waters, it's not to drown you, but to cleanse you.

Suddenly, it became clear what he meant.

I stood up and blew the water from my nose, leaping over to my mother, wading through the thick water and underbrush. I lifted her head from the water with one hand and untied her strains with the other. I almost fell over with relief when she gasped for air. I put her arm around my shoulder and had only made it one step up the embankment when I lost my footing and together we slid back down into the water with a splash.

I was startled by the man looming over us. A man I never wanted to see again. My heart pounded against my ribcage like it was going to leap from my chest and lunge at Richard. The wind picked up, whistling through the trees.

Richard snarled. "Looks like you got yourself a problem there. Although, I'll give you some credit. I half expected to be disposing of corpses by now. Figures that you were both terrible at listening and taking directions. It's not a big shock to me that you two just won't shut up and die when you're told." Richard's words sent fear, but mostly anger, almost twenty-two-years' worth of it, surging through my veins, igniting a fire of rebellion under my skin.

"Hey, Richard?" I asked, looking him right in the eye for the first time in my life. "FUCK YOU!"

His response was to chuckle. "You think you are so brave. But none of that matters when you're dead, sinner," he taunted.

"*Father*, we cannot pick and choose which sins we abide by. You speak out against sinning, but you yourself are a walking contradiction of sin. Of evil. You are guilty of lust, gluttony, wrath, envy, pride, and so much more. I know because I've seen it in the way you drink alcohol like your thirst is unending. I've seen it in the way you've beat and raped my mother. I've witnessed you speak of God's will as if you are the only man in the world who understands it." I laughed at how ridiculous this man really was. "Well, I hate to tell you, but you don't. You don't understand any of it."

"Blasphemy! Blasphemy!" he growled. He pointed a finger down at me. "You little cunt! How dare you!"

I found a sudden freedom in my words, but because I needed time to figure out how I was going to get to myself and my mother out of the swamp alive. "They say the truth will set you free. Well, Father. For your sake. I hope it does just that. Because your truth is that you are a selfish asshole who is going straight to hell."

There we were, laying in the mud, looking up into the eyes of the madman who once dared to call himself my father when he wasn't even a fraction of the man my real father was. My mother slid from my grip. She landed off to the side in the mud with an audible thunk.

Richard pointed at her. "I told your mother a long time ago that I would kill you while she watched if she ever betrayed me. Too bad she isn't conscious to see me keep that promise."

Richard knelt and reached for something in his back pocket. "Goodbye, Daughter."

When you know the end is near you'd think that would be when you're most afraid. It's not. Because as I prepared it to all be over, I couldn't help but to feel proud.

Proud of the woman I'd become. Proud of the relationships I'd made. And proud of the way I was standing up to Richard in my final moments.

Finn would have been proud too.

I made sure I was staring Richard directly in the eyes. If he was going to kill me he was going to have to do it while I disobeyed his stupid rules right to the end. Even the baby gave a defiant first kick against my hand as I protectively covered my stomach.

It made me laugh. I was literally laughing in the face of my own death.

Richard never got a chance to produce whatever weapon he was reaching for because something blunt made contact with his head. There was a dull thud followed by a noise that sounded a lot like a crusty loaf of bread being broken in half.

Richard's stare went blank as he fell face first into the water.

"Mom?"

I looked up to find my mother standing there holding some sort of white rock in her hand. "You're right," she said to Richard's unconscious body. "None of it matters. YOU don't matter."

She continued to stare hatred down at him, cradling the rock in her arms like a trophy. "During your sermons, you frequently spoke about family bonds." She chuckled as she quoted Richard. "I believe it went something like, 'There is no greater bond on this earth than that between a mother and her child. And if someone attempts to destroy that bond? God have mercy on his soul.'"

She stood over him and squared her shoulders. "May God have mercy on your soul, Richard."

"Is he...?" I asked, pausing as I saw the faint rise and fall of his shallow breathing.

My mother shook her head. "I don't think it's that easy." She turned to me. Kneeling she looked me over from head to toe. "Is the baby okay?"

"The baby is fine. I'm fine. But you are the one who's hurt." I pulled gently on her head to take a closer look at the wound.

"It's just a nasty bump," she said, flinching away from my touch.

"It's more than that," I pointed out. "You kept passing out."

"I did earlier. I think it was just an after effect from

whatever he'd held over my nose. But I tell you what, nothing has a way of slapping you awake than the possibility of your imminent demise."

"But you just passed out, just now," I questioned.

She shook her head and winced. "Nope. That was called acting. I took a drama class once. Did you know that?" she asked as she helped me up. I was both impressed and proud and completely in love with my mother.

"No, I didn't know that about you," I said. "But maybe, sometime soon, you can tell me all about it."

We left Richard in the water as we limped over to the boat he had parked between two stumps. It occurred to me that my mother probably did not see the roof of the library collapse.

We needed to get back. We need to see if they had made it out of the library. But first, I had to warn my mother of what we might find when we got back.

Or what we might not find.

I felt like time had stopped around us along with the winds from the storm. The amplified sounds and smells of the swamp from earlier had all died down. It was almost silent. I'm sure if you listened carefully enough you could hear my sorrow.

The words I knew I had to say grew thick in my throat and even thicker as they sprouted roots and wrapped around my heart, squeezing so tightly I didn't know how I was going to breathe again never mind speak.

"Mother," I choked out. "There's something I have to tell you." I shut my eyes tightly.

"What is it?" she asked, sounding every bit as horrified as she should.

A loud vibration rattled through the swamp, shaking every branch of every tree like the beginnings of an earthquake. An airboat emerged, zipping right over a thick layer of brush like it didn't exist. Even in the heavy rain, I could make out the faces on that boat. I would know them from miles away. My soul would recognize them anywhere.

All the feelings I never thought I would experience again, happiness, joy, elation, and love, all came back to me at once. The weight lifted off my chest and I could breathe again. I was so light I felt as if I were floating above my own body.

Critter was driving. Finn was standing at the front.

Both were in one piece.

Both were alive.

CHAPTER 26

FINN

I still had no idea how Sawyer and her mother managed to free themselves from a man who would stop at nothing until he got what he wanted. What he wanted was their lives. By way of either submission or death. Which made me furious beyond reason.

My stomach rolls at the reminder of how close he came to getting what he wanted, of the despair I felt while thinking the absolute worst had already happened.

We were lucky.

Just because I don't know how they managed to free themselves doesn't mean I was surprised. There were never two more determined people on the planet. No one with stronger wills. No one braver.

They might not think so, but they were well-equipped to handle the likes of Richard Dixon.

"I've never been so goddamn scared in my entire life," I told Sawyer as she woke up from a twenty-hour nap. She rolled over took one look at me and smiled like

I meant everything in the world to her. "I can't help but think of what could have happened to you if..."

"Don't. Come here," Sawyer said, stretching out her arm. She rolled over so that we were lying facing one another with our arms and legs intertwined, a lot like we did the first night she spent in my bed. Except this time one of my hands rested on top of our growing baby.

I hadn't gotten much sleep at all. I found my rest in watching my girl sleep, her chest and belly rising and falling with each intake of breath.

"I missed you," Sawyer said sleepily. And although her words were simple, the look in her eyes said so much more.

"Me too," I whispered.

Her eyes widened and met mine. "Richard," she said, suddenly looking panicked.

"He won't hurt you again."

She relaxed into me once more. "What happen to him?"

I twisted my lips. I had a good idea what happened to him, but it wasn't the same as what Critter had SAID happened to him. "Critter told me he was taking Richard back to the jail he escaped from." Saying it out loud didn't make it any more believable.

"Do you think that's what he did?" she asked, knowing Critter just as well as I did.

I sucked in air through my teeth. "I think it's best if we don't know."

"That sounds like something he would say," Sawyer said, placing a hand on my face. I leaned in and kissed her, needing to feel her against me, needing to remind myself that although she was in my arms that she was really here. She was really okay.

"I'm here," she reassured me, knowing exactly what I needed to hear.

"Yes, you are."

She glanced over my head to the nightstand. I turned and noticed she was staring at her dirty clothes in a pile as well as the rock that her mother had been clutching to her chest when we'd found them.

"It was real," she whispered.

"What was real?" I asked, turning back around to face her.

"You see that scarf?" she asked, pointing to the muddied purple piece of cloth on top of the pile. "I had a vision that this blonde woman saved me and she was wearing it. I know it sounds silly but it helped pull me through."

I sucked in a breath, not wanting to think about how scared she must have been but glad she had found comfort in some sense, even if it was in a vision or a dream.

"What's with the rock?" she asked.

I couldn't help the smile that grew on my face. "That's what your mother was holding. That's what she hit Richard over the head with."

"Strange looking rock," she commented.

I sat up to inspect it closer. "You're right. I've never seen a round rock like that around here." I picked it up and turned it over. I almost dropped it when I saw what was on the other side.

"What?" Sawyer asked, scrambling to a sitting position on the bed.

The rock wasn't a rock at all.

It was a skull.

Suddenly something clicked. The purple scarf. The skull.

I envisioned a certain picture hanging over Critter's bar. One where I had my arm draped around Jackie. She was wearing the purple scarf I'd bought her at the craft fair. I even had her initials embroidered in the lining. JC. The exact initials that were peeking through the splotches of filth.

I dropped my head in my hands. At first, I felt my stomach roll like I was going to get sick. I took a deep breath through my nose but it didn't help. This was her. This was Jackie. Suddenly it was two years ago and it was like I'd just lost her all over again. Her death was like a knife to my throat.

"What! What is it?" Sawyer asked again. It was her voice that brought me back to the present. Her voice that reminded me that it wasn't two years ago anymore. I'd almost lost Sawyer. The love of my life. The mother of my child. But I didn't. And something told me the blonde woman in Sawyer's vision was someone familiar to me.

There had been a reason we hadn't found her despite countless searches over the years. And although it sounded ridiculous to even think it, I think she stayed out there for Sawyer...for me.

I felt a warmth grow within me. A sense of completion. Finality. Love. We'd found Jackie...or just maybe, she'd found us.

"Finn?" Sawyer asked again.

I quickly turned the skull back around. "Nothing, I thought a saw a worm on it. It was just a leaf."

"That was an awfully big reaction for a worm," Sawyer said, skeptically. "For someone who grew up in a swamp."

I laid back down on the bed and pulled Sawyer down with me. "Worms are gross," I said, pressing her body against mine. Relishing the feel of her lips as they brushed my jaw.

"No, tell me. Please."

I sighed. "Okay, but it's going to sound a little crazy," I warned her, tracing the freckles around her right eye.

"Lucky for you, I'm used to crazy."

I told her everything and she remained expression-less until the end. "That's not crazy, Finn. That's beautiful."

We remained silent for a while after that. Content with breathing each other in. "Did you know that you are the bravest person I've ever met in my entire life?" I asked, not being able to hold inside how I felt any longer.

"Why do you say that?" she asked, running her hands all over my body like she too cannot believe that I was there. "You are the one who crawled out of a burning building."

"Not so much," I explained. "A rain squall came in at the right time and doused the flames before they could spread."

"I thought you were crushed under the roof," she said, resting her chin on my chest and looking up at me with glassy eyes. I needed to protect her from those kinds of feelings, from the pain.

"No, it was just the part over the storage unit," I reassured her. "I am here. I'm fine." Repeating her same reassurances she just used to comfort me.

I chuckled to myself.

"What's so funny?" she asked, her bright smile lighting up the entire room as well as my heart.

"Here I thought you were the damsel in distress. I was wrong." I cupped her jaw. "As it turns out, you were both the damsel and the knight."

I kissed her deeply and we spent the rest of the night and the following day not more than a few inches from one another. If I had it my way, we'd spend the rest of our lives in bed, but if we did that, I wouldn't get a chance to show Sawyer a surprise I had for her. And as much as I come to learn that she hates surprises, this was one I could not wait to give her.

CHAPTER 27

SAWYER

My mother and I started seeing a therapist together. Eugenia Collins specialized in something she called Religious Trauma Syndrome. She was also a specialist in those who have experienced domestic mental and physical abuse.

And although Finn would probably benefit from talking to someone like Eugenia as well, he insisted he was fine. And because of the way he'd been whistling and skipping around while preparing for the baby to arrive, I was inclined to believe him.

Two days a week we'd make the hour-long drive to her office and we'd each do a session alone and then one together. It was enlightening to learn about how and why we react to things and how blame is so easily placed when it was no one's fault but the person who made us feel this way.

I know my mom was benefiting from it because I could see it in her smile. The softening of her features.

The way she squeezed my hand every time the therapist said something she could relate to. There was pure happiness surrounding her, and again I couldn't help but to think of how brave she truly was.

To be perfectly honest, it wasn't so much the therapy that did it for me, but the time with my mother that I benefited from the most. Most trips I'd drive and while listening to the stories she'd tell and each time I'd learn more about the woman who'd given me life. And each week the life would return more and more to her eyes until I began to know my mother as the rebellious, funny, spunky, stubborn, and loving person that she really was.

She started working with Critter at the bar. Running it, I should say. And between the two of them, they took on the jobs of four people, just like Critter had done, although now he didn't have to do it alone. She looked at home there. At peace. And if you saw the two of them interact, you wouldn't think that two decades passed between them being together. You'd think that they'd been together their entire lives. That's probably because in a way they had never left each other, at least not in their hearts.

Mom was also looking forward to being a grandparent. There were many nights when I heard her bragging about her future grandbaby to customers at the bar.

Speaking of grandparents, I finally got to meet my grandmother. Critter's mother. The shrill voice from the kitchen. A woman I hadn't managed to see in physical form in all the time I'd been in town. When Critter introduced me to her for the first time as her granddaughter, she simply shrugged and said, "I know," before going back to whatever it was she was doing in the kitchen. And For some reason that made my heart smile because not only did I have a family, I had a family that included a crazy anomaly of a grandmother.

Finn and I had finally finished the library. He'd also found his passion. He'd started buying the half-built housing communities scattered around Outskirts. What had started as a bright promise of a future-turned into a ghost town nightmare, Finn had managed to produce an affordable, environmentally friendly, energy-efficient home in its place. The first one was already completed and sold and he was in the process of working on several more.

Finn had also managed to convince a very large car rental company to build their hub just outside of Outskirts by donating the land for the building. Which meant those homes he was building wouldn't go unused and much-needed money would be brought into the town while the town itself would remain small and as charming as ever.

Construction wasn't Finn's passion though. It was people.

ME, our child, and the people of Outskirts.

I'd decided to rotate out pictures from the wall of the bar, with Critter's permission of course, for a display I created in the library, dedicated to the people of Outskirts. Later I planned to incorporate more of the history of the town.

My first display was dedicated to love and friendships. It included an old picture of Critter and my mother. Two pictures of Josh and Miller, one of them arguing and another one of them kissing. A picture of me and Finn, his hands on my belly, as well as a picture of Finn, Miller, Josh, and Jackie when they were just kids. In the center sat a special frame. I'd cleaned the purple scarf that had somehow made its way back with us from the swamp and draped it over the corner of the picture of Finn and Jackie. "Thank you," I whispered, kissing my fingertips and pressing it to the frame.

"What do you call this creation?" Wilfredo asked, coming to stand behind me.

"This?" I beamed, inside and out. "This is something I like to call 'The Outliers.'"

A few moments later, with one snip of the giant scissors Finn and I both held, we officially reopened The Outskirts Public Library to the applause and shouts of our family and friends. "Are you ready?" I asked, pulling on the rope connected to the tarp covering the new sign above the door. We stepped aside to avoid it falling on our heads. Finn laughed until he looked up and read the sign.

Public Library of Outskirts

Dedicated to the memory of Jackie Callahan

Finn's eyes welled up. "You did this?" he asked, looking over at me with wonderment and shock. He smiled down at me and held my face in his hands, planting a kiss on my lips. "Thank you," he said, pulling back slowly. "You are everything."

My insides melted.

Finn had hired a team to extract the rest of Jackie's remains from the swamp. It turns out that the object I'd used to cut myself free from my restraints was a jagged shard of one of her bones. After it was all collected, Jackie's parents asked for her to be cremated and Finn had her ashes sent to them in Tennessee where they'd moved after she passed.

Finn deepened the kiss like he was trying to show me the depths of his gratitude just dedicating the library to Jackie was my way of showing my thanks to her.

Critter cleared his throat nearby. "You two need to cut that shit out."

Finn pulled back but kept an arm around my shoulder. "I've already knocked her up," he argued.

Critter marched toward him and Finn dodged him playfully, bolting into the library. Not one to give up easily, Critter gave chase by way of slow determined stride.

"I guess we're going inside," my mother said, linking her arm with mine.

"Wait," I said. "There is something I want you to have." I unclasped the chain from around my neck and placed the necklace with the sunflower pendant in her hand and closed her fingers around it.

"No," she said, trying to open her fingers back up, but I wouldn't let her.

"This is yours. It was always meant to be yours," I said.

My mother gave a reluctant nod. She opened her hand and held up the pendant. It glistened in the afternoon sun. I helped her clasp it around her neck. When it was secure, she held her hand over it, pressing it closer to her heart.

"You know," she started, "when I found the keys for the storage unit that Richard was keeping my truck and camper in, I was shocked. I wondered why he kept them all those years, but then I realized he was keeping them just like he was keeping me. He didn't want or need them to do what they were made to do, he just wanted to own them. I think in a way they were his trophies for stealing me back. I thought about taking you and jumping in that truck and driving away a million times. But I couldn't risk it, I couldn't risk your safety. I'm just..." she sniffled and wrapped her fingers around the pendant.

"You don't have to, Mom. It's all okay now. There's no need to explain anything. We are here. We aren't going anywhere," I said, grabbing her hand between mine and placing it against my chest.

"I just need you to know that when I bought that land, when I left you that box, when I wrote that letter, I didn't want to kill myself, even though that was the plan. I just couldn't think of another way to get you out. He wouldn't stop unless I was dead and I didn't want you to end up like me when you have so much life in your eyes."

"Mom," I said pulling her against me, relishing the feel of her heartbeat against my own.

"I never wanted to die. I only wanted you to live."

I pulled back. "And I did." I used the heel of my hand to wipe the tears from her face. "And so did you."

WHEN MY MOTHER and I walked into the library, she went to find Critter and I found Finn staring at the display that I'd created. "This is incredible," he said, without taking his eyes from the pictures on the shelf.

"Thank you," I said, feeling proud of what we had accomplished.

Finn turned to me. "I have a surprise for you too," he said, pulling me into his arms. A wicked gleam in his eye.

"There are other people here," I warned between my teeth, squirming against him.

Finn chuckled. "Like I would let any of them stop me," he said. "When the crowd dies down I'll show it to you."

When the last person left and Finn grabbed me by the hand and started leading me away, I was still taken aback. "Oh, it's like a real surprise," I said, following him along. Much to my surprise we passed his Bronco parked in the street and kept on walking.

"Where are we going?" I asked.

"You'll see, it's not far. Are you okay to walk?" Finn asked.

"Yes," I said. The baby had gotten bigger, but I looked a lot more uncomfortable than I was.

We walked hand-in-hand in enjoyable silence. The warmth from his skin pressed firmly against mine as it should be. Although I was much heavier with a big round belly full of baby, my steps were still lighter than they'd ever been.

Finn broke the silence. "Did you know that Critter threatened me again?"

"He did not," I said, clapping my hand over my mouth and trying not to laugh.

Finn nodded. "He sure did. He told me that now that I'm dating his daughter, and because I'd knocked her up without marrying her first, that we aren't to be friends anymore."

"What? But he wasn't serious…was he?"

Finn smiled and the dimple made an appearance. "He said he's moved me up the list and has made me 'enemy number one' in his eyes. If I wasn't the father of his grandchild, he'd disposed of me properly a long time ago." Finn finger quoted the air on the word 'enemy.' "And if I hurt you, he's going to, and I'm quoting him directly now, 'rip out all my vital organs and leave a trail of them on the highway from here to Tuscan.'"

"Points for being creative," I remarked. "What else did he say?"

Finn swayed his head from side to side. "Well, after making me promise to never hurt you, he told me he was going to hold me to that promise."

"That's not so bad."

"At gunpoint."

I laughed. "That sounds more like him." Easily picturing Critter saying those exact words. I loved all his threats. They made me feel special and in a way, I don't think Finn really minded them either.

"So, have you given any more thought into changing your last name?" Finn asked as we turned down a street I'd never been on before.

"Critter and my mom suggested it since she's legally

changed her last name that I should think about doing it too. I think it's a good idea. A fresh start." I admired the large oak trees lining the street. There was also what appeared to be a newly poured sidewalk, the first I'd seen in Outskirts. "I never felt like a Dixon anyway."

Finn bumped my shoulder with his. "That's because you were never a true Dixon, you were a...*Critter*," Finn said, making a face by pushing out his bottom lip to show his teeth and tucking in his chin.

I bumped him back with my hip. "Ha. Ha. I know it's a ridiculous name, but it's my dad's ridiculous name. Which makes it pretty great."

We walked along in comfortable silence again until we stopped at a house at the end of the street. A brand new house from what I could tell. It was white with black shutters and a red front door. "Wow, it's like a two-story version of my little house."

"I know it's not like the three-story Victorian you liked so much but I decided to turn that into a home for women and children."

My shock almost outweighed the extreme happiness that just washed over me like someone had poured a bucket of water on my head. "You own that?"

Finn looked down to the keys in his hand. "Yes," he said like he was reluctant to admit it. "That's where Jackie and I lived. That was our house."

I reached out and brushed my knuckles along the stubble coating his jaw. "It was a beautiful house, but now it's going to be even more beautiful because of your plans for it."

Finn turned and kissed the palm of my hand before spinning me back around to face the house. "Do you like it?" he asked, swinging open the little picket fence and pulling me inside. The flower beds on each side of the door were filled with tall sunflowers that reached halfway up the windows.

"I love it," I said. "Even more than the Victorian." It was the truth. There was something about this house that felt homier. More real. "Is this what you've been working on?" I asked, unable to tear my eyes away from it.

Finn had started taking on some smaller construction projects, but I had no idea he was building houses like this one. "Who is the client??" I was envious of whoever got to live in such a house but proud of Finn for having created something so beautiful. Before he could answer, I added, "Can I see the inside?"

I felt like I needed to at least see it once before it the house changed and became someone's home.

Finn smiled that smile that gave me chills and threaded his fingers with mine. He led me up the front steps opened the door, guiding me through first and following behind.

My mouth fell open. I couldn't speak. I couldn't breathe. It was the most amazing sight I'd ever laid eyes on. "Is this even real?" I whispered.

My state of shock wasn't because of the beautiful grey hardwood floors running from a large living space into a vast and open white kitchen. It wasn't because of the detailed moldings around the windows or the curved iron staircase. It wasn't even because of the big dining room with a huge dark wood table running down the center that could easily fit ten people around it.

No, I was reacting to the thousands of tings covering the entire living room ceiling. They flapped around until Finn closed the door. Although the ceilings were high, the strings were long. As I stepped further into the room, they dangled only an inch or two above my head. "What is all this?" I asked, moving further into the hanging tings until they surrounded me on all sides.

Finn didn't answer, but that was only because the tings answered for him. Every single one of them had the same handwritten message scrawled on them.

WILL YOU MARRY ME?

-FINN

I spun around so fast that if I were any taller I'd be tangled in tings.

Finn was on one knee before me holding out a diamond ring shaped like a sunflower. Light and happiness and promise filled his already handsome bright blue eyes. "So…" he said, making me feel like I was about to burst out of my own skin, "about that last name change?"

Unable to speak real words because joy apparently drains your brain of real coherent thoughts, I joined Finn on the floor, kneeling to face him. When I realized he was still waiting for an answer I nodded so hard I think I shook my words loose. "Yes!" I finally managed to blurt out.

Finn placed the ring on my finger and pulled me against him. Besides, Outskirts, it was my favorite place to be. "I'm so glad we're here, Say," he whispered, his lips finding mine. And whether he meant here as in the house, the town, or as in the place in our relationship, it didn't matter. My response was the same.

"Me too," I whispered.

"I've got one more for you," he said, pulling another ting out of his back pocket and handing it to me along with a black marker.

SHE SAID_____.

-Finn

And of course, through happy tears, I wrote in a great big YES.

In the beginning, Finn and I were just two outliers, each on the cusp of different societies. Together, we found our place and it wasn't in the town. It was in the people of the town. The people who loved us. It was in each other. It was in the new life growing inside of me that we'd created.

It was in family.

Our family.

"And although it's too late now," Finn grinned slyly, "I feel like I still owe you a better lesson on procreation." He ran his hands under my shirt.

"Is that so?" I asked as he unclasped my bra and tossed it to the ground. He made quick work of his own shirt, exposing his defined abs and broad chest.

My mouth went dry. My body hummed.

Finn pushed off his jeans and boxers, exposing his tight butt and muscled abs. I licked my lips at the sight of my beautiful man. I lifted my hips while he peeled off my panties and shorts. He lifted and settled back between my legs where I wanted him most. His hard heat throbbed at my entrance. "Are you ready for your lesson?" he asked, raising his eyebrows wickedly. His voice was raspy and hoarse.

"Yes," I breathed, ready for whatever it is he wanted to give me. "I'm ready."

"Good. Because I can't wait any longer." We were wild and passionate. Needy and desperate.

He pushed himself inside of me with one long thrust that made me gasp, filling me with pleasure while filling my heart with love.

I adjusted around his size, my inner muscles squeezed around him. Finn groaned, the sound making me squeeze him again and again until the pleasure was almost painful. Until there were tears in my eyes and we were the only two people existing on earth.

He held my hands above my head and didn't continue until I was looking him in the eye. "I love you, Say."

"I love you," I replied, looking deeply into his eyes. The feeling between us, the connection we shared, added another log to the fire and our pleasure increased, reaching heights I didn't think possible.

A tear fell from the corner of my eye. It was all too much.

It wasn't enough.

Finn kissed the tear away and began a slow and steady rhythm that had me lifting my hips to meet his thrust for thrust. We somehow flipped from wild sex to passionate love.

"I'm going to make you come now," he said on a low groan. He reached around me to lift me up so he could hit an angle that had me seeing stars with each languid thrust.

"Please," I begged, feeling so close to the edge I was practically living on it.

"Fuck. I feel you. I know you're almost there. Damn, you're so tight around me." He thrust in harder. Over and over again he pushed in and out until his movements became frenzied and we were awash in sensations and feelings.

I couldn't keep track of where he was touching me or where our lips were on my body.

I felt him everywhere.

My skin.

My heart.

My soul.

The muscles in my lower stomach tightened and he reached under my tank top brushing his thumb over my straining nipple which sent a shockwave of pleasure to my core. "I'm I'm…" I couldn't finish my sentence because I was already too far gone. I came in a burst of blinding white light as the immense pleasure exploded within me.

"Holy shit." Finn pushed inside of me one last time until I felt him expand within me, releasing his warmth with a pulse that caused me to shudder one last time as the last of the intense waves washed through me.

The depth of feeling wasn't like it had been the first time in the library. I didn't know how or why pleasure like this existed but all I knew was that Finn had given it to me, and so much more.

A few months later, my father walked me down a makeshift aisle in a field full of sunflowers. During the last moments of daylight, in the exact spot where my parents were married, I held our newborn baby girl between us while Finn and I vowed to always love one another.

Fiercely. Possessively. Crazily.

Always.

The End

EPILOGUE

SAWYER

When we pulled up to Gary's Garage, I furrowed my brow and turned to Finn. "Why are we here?"

"Come on," Finn said, hopping down from the truck. "It's a surprise."

"I thought you knew by now how I felt about surprises?" I asked.

"Well, wifey of mine, I do believe you're holding one of those surprises in your arms right now," he responded playfully.

"You got me on that one," I said, looking down at our daughter who had her daddy's dimple and his bright blue eyes.

Finn bypassed the opened garage bay and took the field to the back of the small building. Finn took Sunny from my arms and cradled her against his chest, my heart skipped a beat the way it always did when I watched him care for our daughter.

"What do you think?" Finn asked, stepping off to the side, revealing the surprise just a few feet away.

I froze. My mouth fell open. I inhaled on a sharp breath, covering my mouth in complete disbelief. "It's....you...I can't believe..." I took a few tentative steps forward, not believing what I was seeing until I was able to run my hand over the glossy new paint on the hood of my mother's once rusty truck and confirm it was real.

It was Rusty all right, except now it was anything but rusty. It had an actual paint color, a robin's egg blue that would've matched...before I could finish the thought, I leaned to the right so I could see beyond the tailgate of the truck.

Sure enough, there was Blue. There were no signs of the storm damage that left it not much more than a twisted pile of scrap metal.

"She runs now," Finn said. "Really well, actually. They've both got a lot of new guts, but deep down. They're still the same 'ole Rusty and Blue you came to love."

"Why?" I asked, turning around. Finn's gaze was fixed on me while he lightly bounced the baby and rubbed circles on her back. "What do you mean why? Because you loved them and I saw how much it broke your heart to lose them. They were your first taste of freedom. I couldn't let you lose them forever."

This man. This wonderful man.

"No. That's not why I love them so much."

"No?" he asked, following behind me as I walked in a circle around Rusty and Blue.

I shook my head and turned back around to face

him. I placed one open palm on Sunny's little back and the other on Finn's chest. " I love them so much because they brought me to you."

Finn leaned down, pressing his lips to mine just as a voice interrupted us. "Here you go, boss," Gary said, tossing Finn the keys. They might not be worth what you spent fixin' them up, but if I got a reaction like the one, you just got, well then, I'd consider polishing up the old Pinto I got in the garage."

When Gary disappeared around the building, Finn tossed me the keys. "They're all yours."

"Thank you," I breathed, wrapping my arms around Finn, careful of Sunny in his arms. "You made them live again. Thank you."

"Just like you made me live again," he said, lightly pinching my chin and placing a chaste kiss on my forehead. I closed my eyes and leaned into his lips, breathing in his fresh woodsy scent. Tingles. Tingles everywhere. "Now come on, we've got a lot of road to cover tonight."

"Tonight?"

"Yes, tonight." Finn opened the passenger door and made a grand sweeping gesture with his arm. "Since these belong to you, I would normally let you drive, but since you're still learning, and technically don't have a driver's license, I will do the honors for now."

"That works," I said, getting in while Finn buckled Sunny in the car seat he'd already had installed in the small back seat.

"Where are we going?" I asked, excitedly.

"My parents' place. I figured since we've got all this

family now, we better start visiting more often with grandbaby or we'll never hear the end of it."

Finn turned the key. The engine roared to life. No coughs. No sputtering.

The sound vibrated through me. I squealed with delight and ran my hands over the dashboard.

"Are you ready, family?" Finn asked, looking in the backseat at Sunny then back at me.

"We are."

When it comes down to it, Blue and Rusty were the same truck and camper at heart; now they were just shinier and in perfect working condition.

They'd been made new again. Rescued from ruin.

Reborn into a life they were always meant to live.

Just like Finn. Just like me.

Just a couple of outliers.

BONUS SCENE

CRITTER

Frankly, I'd waited too goddamned long to have Richard in this position to be turning him over to the authorities. He'd be meeting an authority all right, but I'm positive the one he'll be seeing is located a lot further south than The Outskirts Police Station.

"You know, as a kid, I woke up on Christmas morning with a butterfly feeling in my stomach. Excitement over what present I might have gotten. What might be waiting there for me under the tree." I leaned against the tree that was to be Richard's final resting place and looked down at him. "I'm kinda feeling that way right now."

He struggled against his restraints. "Oh, come on. No need to struggle. I was an Eagle Scout and served three tours with the ole red white and blue. Ain't no way you're getting yourself out of those knots."

Richard yelled into the cloth gag I'd shoved in his mouth. "Don't even worry, Richard. I'm not gonna kill ya." I lit a cigar and tucked the lighter back into my shirt pocket. "Promised the missus I wouldn't, and unlike you, I keep my promises. Also, unlike you, she was always my wife. Never yours. Same goes for my daughter."

Richard bucked again, cursing up a muffled storm. I chuckled. "Didn't know that, did ya? Yeah, we were married. Legally, unlike that bullshit voodoo wedding y'all have over there up in the crazy town you pass off as a church."

I took a deep breath through my nose. "You smell that? Don't you love that swamp air? That sulfur smell after a good hurricane? It's like the world is cleansing itself of all of the dead things it doesn't need anymore." I looked down at Richard whose eyes were bugging out of his skull. I ruffled his hair. "See where I'm going with this?"

I was kind of disappointed this all had to come to an end. I was enjoying myself too much. But I couldn't stay. I had to get back to Caroline. To my family.

"This feels good. Satisfying. So satisfying, in fact, I feel the need for a pre-revenge cigarette. But since I didn't have one and didn't smoke 'em, this cigar will have to do."

A boat approached in the distance. Slowly, quietly. No lights.

Showtime.

I crouched down in front of Richard. "You took my wife and daughter and didn't even have the decency as a man to give them a good life. You are as low as they come. Any last words?"

I pulled out his gag.

"You'll go to hell for this," Richard seethed.

I shoved the gag back in his mouth. I stood up and took a puff of my cigar. I shrugged as the boat drew closer.

"Then I guess I'll see you there." I patted Richard on the shoulder. "Save me a seat on the bus." I smiled and set my cigar in my mouth. "And buy me a fan, would ya? I hear it's hot as fuck down there."

Richard's eyes snapped to the man dressed in all black who hopped from the boat. The blonde devil himself, Jake Dunn, appraised his prey, barely sparing me a glance. He didn't say a word, the kid never did, but he gave me a curt nod and that was my cue to leave.

"Sorry, I can't stay to watch the show, but I'm sure Jake here is gonna make sure that you're well taken care of while he slowly secures your ticket down south."

Richard screamed behind his gag as Jake approached.

With Jake at the helm there was no doubt that Richard Dixon was about to finally get what he deserved, and so much more.

"Make sure it hurts," I called over my shoulder, hopping on my boat and starting the engine.

"It will," Jake said in a tone so low it was almost inaudible.

I took another puff on my cigar and waved a goodbye to Richard with my middle finger. "I'll pray for you," I shouted as I took off to the muffled screams and moans of Richard getting the first taste of what Jake was about to dish out.

"Rot in hell, motherfucker," I muttered to myself as I maneuvered the boat through the thick brush on my way back home to my wife and daughter.

My family.

After all, I had my work cut out for me with them. Two decades is a lot of time to make up for. Christmases and birthdays. Anniversaries. I was already planning all the makeup days in my head.

After that night, I decided I was never going to let the thought of Richard steal another happy moment or another happy thought from me. He'd already taken so much. He wasn't getting any more. Not a single thought. Not from me.

The only exception was when I couldn't sleep at night. Then my thoughts would drift to him. I'd lie awake with my arms wrapped around Caroline and I'd think of how Richard met his end. After a short while, it would solve my lack of sleep problem and I'd drift off like a baby drunk on his mama's milk.

Richard's death was the new counting sheep.

And with my family all home and safe, I never slept better.

BONUS SCENE 2

SAWYER

"What's that?" I asked, turning my head to the side so I could better hear the music coming from behind the ordinary looking doors.

"That?" Finn smiled and raised my hand to his mouth to place a chaste kiss over my knuckles. Chaste or not, it still made the hair on my arms stand on end. "Is the sound of religion number nine."

"Religion number nine sounds amazing," I admitted, moving toward the door like the music was moving my feet for me.

"Wait until you hear how it sounds from the inside," Finn replied, opening the double doors.

The melody exploded all around us. Immediately goosebumps broke out all over my skin. A feeling of pure joy surged in my chest.

We sat in the back row so as not to disturb the two-dozen or so other people in attendance.

The inside of the church wasn't very church-like at all. It was void of stained glass or depictions of the stations of the cross or the Virgin Mary. The main area of worship was a simple yellow room with several rows of white folding chairs on each side of the makeshift aisle. The walls were decorated with brightly colored children's finger paints, along with bulletin boards with various flyers overflowing with pinned announcements.

The music, the product of a small band set up in the front corner of the room. A young woman wearing ripped jeans and a Guns-N-Roses tank top, who looked to be about my age, was singing into a microphone on a stand with her eyes closed. Her voice was melodic. Haunting. I could feel her words in my soul as she swayed to the music she herself was helping to create. I was immediately mesmerized by her voice and by her words.

We sing for love and love alone.
   Love is what will always bring us home.
   We live for light, but darkness still looms.
   It's our light within that will chase away the doom.

"Wow," I whispered.

Finn answered in his usual way. A squeeze of my hand to let me know he was there.

When the song was over the pastor spoke about love and loss to the crowd. It was so different than what I was used to. I always felt like I was being disciplined during a service for all the wrong I hadn't even known I'd committed. This was positive. Engaging. Like having a conversation rather than being yelled at.

The pastor never stood at the front of the crowd or behind a podium. He instead walked up and down the aisle making eye contact with each person in attendance, including myself and Finn.

When the service concluded and the room was almost empty, Finn brought me up to meet the pastor.

"I'm going to let you two talk," Finn said, excusing himself to take a call outside.

The pastor motioned at in the front row in the now empty room. He started by introducing himself as Pastor Dave, but 'you can just call me Dave.'

"Finn told me about your situation and a little about your background. He also says that you're between faiths right now," Dave said. His words were calm and clear and completely without judgment.

I laughed. "I guess I never thought of it that way, but yes, in a way I am between faiths. I'm writing a blog about different religions, their history, and what faith really is and what it means to different people. I figured the best way to write about them is to experience them for myself."

Dave's smile was kind, showcasing the fine lines around his mouth. I guessed him to be somewhere in his late forties. "I think that's fantastic. Well, the short version of our little congregation is that we are an interfaith church, which means that we don't accept any one faith is the 'right' faith or the one 'true' faith. What we do here is recognize that we are all brothers and sisters on this earth and that we are all in this together. That's what we celebrate at our services. People are too busy with the 'right and wrongs' of religion. That's where they've got it all wrong. They're too caught up in the details. The minutia of it all. We focus on the goodness in our hearts because God lives in our hearts, not in the details."

"I've never thought of it that way," I said.

We talked for another fifteen minutes or so. After which I thanked him for his time and contemplated his words. Finn joined us at the door just as I had said my goodbyes.

"Pastor Dave?" I asked.

He turned back around. "Yes?"

"Do you think it would be okay if I came to the service again next week?"

"We'd like nothing more than to have you, Miss Sawyer."

I smiled, and Finn grabbed my hand. "That went well, huh?" he asked, planting a kiss on the top of my head.

"Yes, yes it did," I responded. "It went better than I'd thought. I'd pictured religion and faith in my head as this monstrous thing for so long. This was...happiness. A celebration. I didn't know it could be like this."

"Neither did I," Finn said, gazing down at me with heat in his eyes. I was pretty sure he wasn't talking about the church. My entire body grew warm.

Finn continued walking with his arm draped around my shoulder, and the buzz of our connection humming between us.

I didn't know if I'd become a member of the church for the long term. All I knew was that Pastor Dave was right. God is the love in our hearts.

And my heart?

I looked up to Finn again and thought about our little girl who was the spitting image of her father.

It was overflowing with the stuff.

"Did I tell you that I decided on a name for the blog?" I asked Finn as we walked hand in hand. It had completely slipped my mind.

"No, what did you decide?"

I stopped and turned to face him, craning my neck to look in his beautiful blue eyes.

"The Religious Adventures of Sawyer and Finn."

A PREVIEW OF UP IN SMOKE

A KING SERIES NOVEL

Frankie

I steel my nerves by taking a deep breath.

"What the fuck do you think you're doin'?" Smoke bellows as I appear before him wearing practically nothing.

"What?" I ask, using my most innocent voice. I glance down at my sheer black bra and matching panties. "You don't like what you see?" I sway my hips as I speak and press my teeth into my bottom lip.

Smoke scoffs, although I can see from the way his nostrils flare that I'm affecting him. "You're...cute." I know he means it as an insult. It certainly feels like one. "But I like women, not little girls like you." He waves his hand up and down my body dismissively.

And while his words say one thing, his eyes are telling me something completely different. He gives my body another look, licking me up and down with his gaze, lingering on the scrap of fabric between my legs then up to the sheer triangles doing nothing to hide my nipples which rebel against me. Smoke watches them as they harden under his glare. He tries to hide his smirk, but I see it before he can cover it.

"I'm not a little girl," I argue. I take another step closer gathering my long silky hair over one shoulder. "And you're lying because if you didn't like what you see, you wouldn't be eye fucking me right now." I try to remain confident, keeping up the façade of the seductress. I was terrified that he was going to call my bluff at any moment.

"Such big words for such a little girl," Smoke said flippantly. He shifted on the couch spreading his long-sculpted legs just a bit wider, adjusting the tight denim at his knees.

"I'm not a little girl!" I shouted, taking a step forward in challenge. I stopped mid-step, reminding myself that my plan wasn't to fight with him, it was to seduce him, and in turn, possibly save my own life.

I hoped.

Smoke's perfect thick lips turn upward on the ends. He looks smug and infuriates me. Because, if this was a fight, he knows he just won the first round. My confidence wavers and suddenly standing in front of him feels more like exposure than seduction. But I can't let him see my hesitation.

My life depends on it.

"What game are you playing at here?" he asks. I hate the amusement in his voice. More than that, I hate how my body responds to that voice.

The need to press my thighs together as my core clenches is overwhelming. I attempt to do it subtly, trying to cover the movement with what I think is a sexy sway of my hips. It doesn't work. Smoke notices. His chest lightly shakes with silent laughter. He leans his elbow on the armrest of the couch and rests his head on the tips of his fingers. The other arm is resting on his thigh, his hand falling just below the enormous bulge in his jeans.

I willed myself not to stare at it as he continued. "'Cause, no matter what happens, Princess," he lowers his voice to a throaty whisper. "You're gonna lose."

"That's what you think," I say in my most sultry sounding voice. I'm not sure what game I'm playing. No, I do know. I'm playing a game where the prize could be my freedom.

My life.

"This won't change anything. I mean it," Smoke barks. There is no trace of humor in his tone.

I don't respond. Smoke could tell me he doesn't want me all night long, but his dilated pupils and dark-ening eyes tell another story. One of lust. Need.

I have to do this. I'm running out of time.

All he needs is a little push.

I unhook my bra, dropping it to the floor. Smoke watches me intently. His nostrils flare. He runs his tongue over his lower lip as he drinks me in.

I shiver.

He's quiet for a moment. Fear spikes through me at the thought that I've lost my only chance. He glances back up to meet my eye like he has come to some sort of conclusion. "All right, Princess." Smoke's wicked smirk is back. I broke with the scar raises when he says, "You think you can handle a man like me?"

The way he says it drips with the challenge. With promise.

With a warning.

I take a bold step toward him. I make no move to cover my naked breasts. I'm calling his bluff, just like he's calling mine. A thrill shimmies its way to my very core, no doubt a result of being both excited and alarmed over what might happen.

"Then come on, Princess," Smoke says, unbuckling his belt and unzipping his jeans. His tight black boxers stretch over his straining erection. I can see a flash of flesh beneath the thin fabric.

He extends one last warning. "A fuck won't buy your freedom. I'm a lot of things, but a liar isn't one of them. You wanna fuck me?" The way he says the word fuck sends shivers up my spine. My nipples harden further, and I pretend it's because of the air skating across my naked skin. "You want me to bend you over the arm of this couch and show you how a real man fucks?" He nods in agreement to his own words. "Then let's go. But you're going to regret it, because as I've said, it changes nothing."

I smile like his words didn't send spasms of fear and disappointment pulsating through my chest. Whether he was right or not doesn't make a difference. It's my last chance.

Maybe my only chance.

I approach the couch and kneel before him, spreading my fingers over his jean covered thighs, pretending like I'd done this kind of thing a million times before.

I hope he can't feel me shaking.

Smoke grabbed my wrist roughly, lifting it off his leg. He snarled. "This isn't a fucking joke, little girl. I know you think you're smart, and I know there are a lot of motherfuckers out there that will fall for your bullshit, but in case you haven't noticed, I ain't like other guys. I see right through this act of yours. I ain't buying it." He leaned forward his face inches from mine. He smells like leather and fresh soap. "You can't buy your freedom with pussy, because your freedom ain't for sale."

"It's not an act," I lie, defensively with my teeth gnashed together. I try to yank my wrist from Smoke's grip, but he squeezes tighter, his fingernails biting into my flesh.

I gasp when a bolt of heat passes between us. We both lower our eyes and stare at the place where his hand has my wrist trapped, and I wonder if he feels it too. The electric-type current running across our skin and deeper.

Smoke growls, releasing me so suddenly I fall back onto the floor. "Have it your way, Princess," he says bitterly. His eyes are dangerously dark. His eyes are heavily lidded. There's a crackle in the air that wasn't there a moment ago. He leans back on the couch, looks down to his jeans that are still hanging open then back up to me. "Take out my cock and ride me," he demands.

Shit.

I swallow hard. I'm panicked. I'm turned on. And I have no idea what I'm doing or how I'm going to get out of this.

Do I *want* to get out of this?

There's no time to answer my own question.

Smoke's watching me. Waiting. My pulse is racing loudly in my ears. He shifts, pressing his lips together as if he can hear it too. I slowly rise to my knees once again. I don't think, I just move—pushing my panties down my legs and pulling them off my feet.

I'm now completely naked. Exposed to the enemy.

The nakedness and the way he looks at me. Carnal. Primal. It wouldn't have bothered me so much before, but now I felt more vulnerable than ever because Smoke knows of my intentions.

And he's about to find out all there is to know about my body.

I reach up and hook my fingers into the waistband of his jeans and start to snake them down over his narrow hips. My fingertips tingle when they connect with the warm muscled skin of his torso. I hate myself for wanting to push up his shirt and run my palms along every inch of his chest and abs.

I flash him a smug smile of my own. Smoke watches my every move with laser-like interest, daring me to follow through.

The fact that I know things he doesn't makes me feel powerful even though I'm the one on my knees.

Everything I've ever told him has been a lie.

Every. Single. Thing.

Since that very first day.

The day he abducted me.

Up in Smoke is available for preorder and coming soon.

THE OUTSKIRTS DUET

Finn & Sawyers Story

THE OUTSKIRTS

THE OUTLIERS

KING SERIES

King & Doe's Story (Duet)

KING

TYRANT

Bear & Thia's Story (Duet)

LAWLESS

SOULLESS

Preppy & Dre's Story (Triplet)

PREPPY PART ONE

PREPPY PART TWO

PREPPY PART THREE

Up In Smoke: Coming early 2018

STANDALONES

Jake & Abby's Story

THE DARK LIGHT OF DAY, A KING SERIES PREQUEL

Rage & Nolan's Story

ALL THE RAGE, A KING SERIES SPIN OFF

Visit T.M. Frazier's AMAZON page for a listing of all her available books.

www.amazon.com/author/tmfrazier

ACKNOWLEDGMENTS

Thank you to Mr. Frazier for your constant encouragement. I couldn't do this without you. Writing. Life. The whole nine yards. <3

Thanks to Ellie from Love-N-Books for the edits and shit.

Thanks to Becca from Evident Ink for being the Swift to my Sheeran. Thank you for reminding me that people have feelings. Thank you for putting up with my impossible deadline and for not being a total dick about it.

Thank you to Jenn Watson for your mad PR skills and your friendship. #CaliforniaLove

Thank you to my agent, Kimberly Brower of Brower Literary & Management.

Thank you to Wander Photography for the great cover photo. Margaritas on Mr. Frazier!

Thank you as always to all my readers in Frazierland. What an amazing group of readers. I am so grateful to have all of you in my life.

Thank you to all the bloggers and readers who shout from the rooftops about their love of my books. YOU are everything.

Love,

T.M.

ABOUT THE AUTHOR

T.M. FRAZIER

T.M. Frazier is a *USA TODAY* Bestselling Author best known for her **KING SERIES**.

She was born on Long Island, NY. When she was eight years old she moved with her mom, dad, and older sister to sunny Southwest Florida where she still lives today with her husband and daughter.

When she was in middle school she was in a club called AUTHORS CLUB with a group of other young girls interested in creative writing. Little did she know that years later life would come full circle.

After graduating high school, she attended Florida Gulf Coast University and had every intention of becoming a news reporter when she got sucked into real estate where she worked in sales for over ten years.

Throughout the years T.M. never gave up the dream of writing and with her husband's encouragement, and a lot of sleepless nights, she realized her dream and released her first novel, The Dark Light of Day, in 2013.

She's never looked back.

FOLLOW T.M. FRAZIER
FACEBOOK: @TMFRAZIERBOOKS
INSTAGRAM: @T.M.FRAZIER
TWITTER: @TM_FRAZIER
AMAZON:
www.amazon.com/author/tmfrazier
NEWSLETTER SIGN UP:
http://www.subscribepage.com/tmfraziernewslettersignup
FACEBOOK GROUP:
www.facebook.com/groups/tmfrazierland

For business inquiries please contact
Kimberly Brower of Brower Literary & Management.
www.browerliterary.com

Made in the USA
Lexington, KY
20 December 2017